DEVIL MAY CARE

MAX HENRY

DEVIL MAY CARE
Copyright © 2015 Max Henry
Published by Max Henry

All rights reserved. No part of this book may be reproduced or transmitted in any form, including electronic or mechanical, without written permission from the publisher, except in the case of brief quotations embodied in critical articles or reviews.
This is a work of fiction. Names, characters, businesses, places, events, and incidents are either the products of the author's imagination or used in a fictitious manner. Any resemblance to actual persons, living or dead, or actual events is purely coincidental. Max Henry is in no way affiliated with any brands, songs, musicians, or artists mentioned in this book.
This book is licensed for your personal enjoyment only. This book may not be re-sold or given away to other people. If you would like to share this book with another person, please purchase an additional copy for each person you share it with. If you are reading this book and did not purchase it, or it was not purchased for your use only, then you should return it to the seller and purchase your own copy.
Thank you for respecting the author's work.

Published May 2015, by Max Henry **maxhenryauthor@outlook.com**
Edited by: Lauren McKellar
Cover & Formatting by: Cover Story Book Designs

Note to Readers

Devil May Care is a **companion novella** to the Butcher Boys series and **needs** to be read in sequence to be **fully appreciated**.

If you haven't already, please read **Devil You Know**, followed by **Devil on Your Back** before you start this story.

Thank You

Want to hang out with like-minded chicks?

Jump into **Max's Minxes** on Facebook!

www.facebook.com/groups/346994535466425/

He in his madness prays for storms,
and dreams that storms
will bring him peace.

- Leo Tolstoy

prologue

Madness by itself can be endearing; in that moment of complete release from the world and everything you're *supposed* to be, a person can find the ultimate freedom.

A sense of belonging. Happiness.

There's no expectation, no right or wrong, just the simple question: what is it *you* want to do? Things happen because you choose for them to, and they happen for a reason—to bring you reward. You don't answer to anyone, and you sure as fuck don't have to explain yourself, either. Somebody gives you grief? Then remove them.

It's that simple.

After a while, you begin to look at the people around you not by their emotional value, but by what they can do for you. That friend you used to hang around and shared some epic memories with? Yeah, well he's now the guy who owns a holiday house you can access when you need to lay low. The old dude at the bar who would share his war stories with you? He's just a guy with the early stages of dementia—one you can manipulate into being an alibi.

You become the music maker. And the world is your

fucking orchestra.

Yet every now and then, you stumble over a bump in the road—a person you haven't seen for a while, or some evidence you missed on your last job. Little skipped notes in your grand opus of life. Being the control freak that you are, these things get to you. Your manic soul loses focus, or direction—only for a heartbeat—and the orchestra stumbles. The bows screech over the gut-strings, crying like banshees as you lose control of the people around you. The audience looks on; grim expressions in place as your players fumble and stall in their attempt at saving the master work. Yet the chaos continues to unfold. The baton is dropped from your hand, and the sour notes crawl over your flesh like parasites, reminding you how you were doomed to fail from the very start. The music no longer masks your inadequacies, but emphasizes them. And then the worst happens ... you realize there is something greater than madness—losing your mind within the psychotic world you live in.

Going crazy when you're already insane.

Fingernails scratch at flesh, and you tear yourself apart searching for the broken piece of yourself. The audience watches in silence, their faces a mixture of disgust and pity as you claw yourself to pieces, tearing flesh from bone while the ear-piercing tones of your failing orchestra swirl about you. A steel determination drives you, telling you that somewhere deep inside the body you're currently ripping apart is a small, damaged element, which once removed will restore your beautiful world. That the symphony can again be magnificent.

And yet, somewhere amidst the gore and the carnage, you

realize that the orchestra is no longer the main attraction—you are. The audience is standing, leaving, certain you've finally found the end—that nobody could survive this. And most alarmingly, you agree. The chaotic noise dims about you as you fall to your knees and cry, realizing in your most desolate hour of destruction that there never was any peace in madness.

That the only person you were fooling … was you.

homecoming

Two more turns. There are two fucking corners left before we reach the shithole I swore I wouldn't step foot in again. *I can do this.* I've left before—I can leave again.

Not a word has been spoken in the car since we left King and the others at the park—not as we entered the freeway, not as we exited and made a random stop-off, and certainly not as Eric stepped out and shoved something large and heavy into the trunk of the Dodge.

Something screaming.

I close my eyes and tune into the distressed calls of our cargo, relishing the melody that has finally drowned out the fucking voice in my head. All the bastard did was criticize and insult me. I know that shit. He knows I know that shit. There's no reason to rehash the obvious, and it's exactly why I shove that lippy fucker into the darkest corner of my mind. If only he'd shut up though. If only he'd leave me alone.

You're such a failure . . .

No wonder nobody wants you . . .

Utterly useless . . .

I turn my head and look at my father. He's a man who

owns his wealth, owns his status, and damn well exudes the arrogance that got him where he is today. I bet the asshole's never had to deal with the kind of demons I live with. He wouldn't be so well put together if he did. Despite a few silver strands invading his perfectly-styled dark hair, and a few extra lines around his eyes that hint at his age, he's the picture of style. He's grace and charm. The wolf in sheep's clothing.

A professional fucking liar.

"Are you going to share with me why we have a passenger?" I ask.

He turns toward me and glances at the seats between us, as though looking directly through them to our captive. His lip curls with disgust. "All in due course."

Right—I tend to forget how close he holds his cards to his chest. Everything's all a big fucking secret until he decides he needs your input. *Using, lying fucktard.* We resume ignoring one another, and I choose to watch the droplets of rain trickle over the window while we speed toward our final destination. They struggle against the current, trying to keep themselves together despite the odds of survival being against them. Much like the girl in the back.

He doesn't really want you. You're a liability, and you know what he does with those . . .

Yeah, you can go shove your opinion where the sun doesn't shine, asshole.

I like to think of the voice in my head as my conscience; he's a clean-cut version of me, sitting in the control room of my mind and cursing at every stupid thing I've done . . . and I do a lot of those. My teeth grit painfully and I screw my eyes tight, trying to force him to quiet. I don't want or need to be reminded of why I left my father's home to begin with. The man has never shown me a singular ounce of compassion, care or love. In my school years, I would watch other kids get picked up by their father at the end of the day, or have their old man cheer them on from the sidelines while they played sport on the weekend. But me? At first it was my mother coming to get me at the end of the day, but after she died, it was Eric's predecessor. I was picked up, chauffeured, and taken wherever the fuck I pleased by a guy who knew me only as a job to be completed. The only thing cheering me on when I scored a home run was a dark car in the parking lot that all the other families would steer clear of.

Where was my father? He was far too fucking busy paying off some bureaucratic fat-cat, negotiating a shipment, or cutting the fingers off some fucker that had looked the wrong way at his latest whore. He was, and is, far too obsessed with his empire to give a shit about his own flesh and blood.

I'm nothing but an asset, a tool, and when those things get worthless, what do you do? Replace them. And he has—with three half-siblings that I've never met.

You should have died with her...

Like fuck I should have. The devil in my head can go suck it. I'm here for a purpose, for a fucking reason, and that is to shame my father and prove to him his first-born son is better and smarter than he'll ever be. If I'm going to die, it'll be with that heartless bastard begging at my feet for forgiveness.

Like that would ever happen...

The girl's screaming becomes pleading, and finally a dull sob as the car slows outside the gatehouse that guards the entrance to my father's property. The two-inch reinforced-steel gate before us sits as a centerpiece for the sixteen-foot stone wall that seals my father's residence. Paranoia would be a light way of describing my old man's distrust of the world.

I run my eye over the ivy that covers most of the wall as Eric speaks to the guard, and the blockade slides open with a graunch. We soon find ourselves cruising to a stop at the entrance to the large house. The monstrosity before me is just as audacious as I remember—a mansion of stone and iron amongst the softly manicured gardens of my mother. The place is renaissance in appearance, thanks to the original owner's obsession with British royalty, and my mother did a pretty good job of designing a garden that suited the look: trimmed hedges, large oaks and marble statues. My old man would never think to do something so beautiful. Not when he could be spending time ruining somebody's life.

The muffled sobbing continues in short hiccups from the back while I watch Eric and my father exit the car. They stand outside my window and discuss something in length before they remember they have passengers.

That's right, fuckers. I can't get out of this vehicle on my own.

Eric turns to face my window, and lifts the handle. I shunt my feet hard against the door, forcing him back with a grunt.

"About fuckin' time you let me out," I grumble, placing my boots on the ground and standing.

My head whips forward with a sharp sting. The impact of my father's hand has me right at home. It's as though I never left.

"You going to untie me, or what?" The assholes have no reason to keep me bound up; my father's guards will ensure I don't get far if I try and run.

"Eric, take those ropes off." My old man wanders to the back of the car while his bodyguard does as told. The old bastard smiles sadistically at Eric and I, and then raps his knuckles on the trunk. "Hello?"

"Let me out, you motherfucker!"

He grins, and wiggles his eyebrows as if to say 'watch this.' The asshole saunters to the front of the car and pops the trunk. The girl's legs propel from the gap, and she wrestles to get her body from the car. My father takes hold of a slender wrist, and yanks her out into the cool night air. There's a momentary pause as she cases her surroundings, and then she does it.

She tries to run.

My father's arms circle her as she pushes off. "Not safe to be out at this time of night alone, dear."

Her cries echo across the gardens while I push against what's left of the ropes around my arms, eager to get in on the action. Eric squeezes a firm hand around my shoulder as a warning. "Yeah, I get it," I mutter. "Just hurry the fuck up."

Blonde curls bounce in the moonlight as the girl continues to wrestle against my father's hold. "Settle down, bitch!" he growls, trying to re-capture her flying arms. He manages to connect a fist to the side of her face, and it works as far as snapping her senses about.

She stands, stunned, palm to her cheek and mouth open in shock. Even in the relative dark, her skin appears golden.

She's showing plenty of it off in a fucking short pair of denim cut-offs and a cropped T-shirt. Tattoos snake up her arms, and a spray of delicate flowers adorn her left calf. My gaze trails down her body, over her small breasts, curvy hips and long legs, until finally settling on the one detail of her attire which has me growing hard—cherry-red Doc Marten boots, loosely laced.

She looks like she could be fun . . .

For once, I'm inclined to agree with that asshole in my head. She does look like fun.

Eric drops the last of the rope from my arms, and I stretch them out before me, popping the kinks out of my shoulders. My father opens his mouth to spout off some more shit at the girl, but I cut him short by taking a huge stride forward, and grabbing her about the waist. *This one's mine.* Her fate was sealed the minute I laid eyes on that tight little body all covered in ink.

She squeals as I throw her over my shoulder, beating me with her tiny fists and kicking those boots out in front of me. "Dibs," I holler, taking off up the steps with her bouncing on my shoulder.

A deep, rumbling chuckle behind me threatens to ruin the oddly good mood I'm in. For the first time in his fucking life, my father laughs at something humorous I've done. I could drop the girl where I stand right now, and rip his fucking face off for it. It's a bit late to be showing me any sort of friendly interaction now. *Asshole.* He's fucking lucky my dick's got other priorities.

The girl screams blue murder, calling me every name under the sun, but I continue through the house toward the east wing and my old room. Her fists have turned to nails, and she claws and rips flesh from my back. The pain is incredible, and a huge fucking turn-on. *Easy, girl.*

I toss her higher on my shoulder mid-stride to reposition her properly, and she grunts out a rough breath. "Put me down, you fucking asshole!"

Nuh-uh. I chuckle, and kick the bedroom door shut behind us and flick the light on. As if I'd give in that easy. Those cherry boots make a heavy thud as I set her down, and she immediately fakes left and then tries right to get around me. I fling an arm about her waist as she lunges for the door, and haul her in front of me in one sweeping motion.

What should we do next? The devil in my mind rubs his hands together.

Setting her down in front of me, I take a step back to give her the once-over. "Where you thinkin' of goin', sweet-heart?" Her curves are all perfectly proportioned, and her tits strain against the cropped tee.

The girl shuffles on the spot, and then pops a hip before frowning. "Where do you think I'm going?" She flicks her head to toss those golden curls over her shoulder, revealing a slender neck—also tattooed. "I'm going home, you fucking bastard."

Yep—most definitely a hot piece of ass.

"Wrong," I snap, startling her. "You aren't going anywhere. Not now I've got you." The corner of my mouth curls into a lopsided grin.

"Are you fucking mad?"

I stare blankly at her. *Why yes, yes I am.*

"Do you have any idea what my father will do when he

finds out?" she continues. "He'll fucking tear this place apart and murder you sons-of-bitches in the process." Her small fists clench at her sides.

Please, go right ahead. Fuck, I'd go so far as to open the front door for the bastards . . . then join in the carnage.

She stomps her foot like a child, her face contorted with rage. The silky curls bounce on her shoulders while she continues to scream her frustrations at me. "You have no right to take me!"

I have to give it to her—the girl has spark.

"Who the fuck are you, anyway?" she spits, jabbing at my cut. Her boots clomp around me, and I keep a keen eye on her to make sure she doesn't run again. The footfalls stop directly behind me, and she gasps.

A sharp pain stabs inside my ear as her screaming resumes. "You're one of us? You're a fucking Saint?"

One of us? My cocks goes limper than a wet noodle. This game isn't so fun anymore. I whirl on her, causing her to back into a wall, and take her jaw in my hand. Turning her head side to side I look her over, and frown when the pieces don't quite mesh.

"Why do you look familiar?" I ask.

"I could say the same thing," she hisses. "What I really want to know is, why am I here if you're a motherfuckin' Saint?"

Dirty mouths are only good for dirty things . . .

I close my eyes with her jaw still in my grasp, tell the devil in my head to quit with the fucking suggestions, and take a deep breath. "Baby, you got to stop swearin' and fightin' me or you'll find yourself with my dick in your mouth."

She snorts—actually laughs at the suggestion. This girl has no idea what trouble she's playing with. I reach down and flick the buckle on my belt, and smirk as she stills.

Good girl.

"Maybe you're used to the big talk, darlin', but when I threaten somebody I'm dead serious." My gaze roams over her tight little body once more, and I internally slap the shit out of myself for not going through with it. "Now, you best be tellin' me exactly who you are and what the fuck my father wants with you."

I drop my hold on her, my hand itching to reach lower on her tanned body, and she tilts her chin up before answering. "I'm Dana Carlyle, and my father is Bobby Carlyle, although I'm sure you know him better as Judas."

"Fuck, bitch. I know who Bobby Carlyle is." What I don't know is what the fuck my old man is up to stealing a Saint's daughter? Her dad's the president of the southern chapter, which makes her a club princess, and my old man's fucking kidnapped her. "Why has my father lifted you?" I ask.

"You tell me, champ. What the fuck *is* your dad doing bringing me here if his son is a Saint?"

I pin her under a direct glare. Her lips fall into a pout while she shifts between feet. "What?"

"Just didn't recognize you, is all. I mean, I knew Judas had two daughters—just he kept you pretty hidden when I was there. You only came into the club for family get-togethers. Shit, I can't even remember what you looked like." I sweep a hand the length of her. "It sure as fuck wasn't like this."

"Yeah, well, that was a while ago," she says, crossing her arms so her boobs pop. "I grew up, and priorities changed for him."

I force myself to look away from her cleavage before I start envisaging my dick between those mounds. *Too late.* "You must know who I am then, right?"

Her eyes crinkle with a cruel smile, and she nods. "Being you're Carlos's son, you must be Sawyer. I heard lots about you." Her gaze flicks to my groin and it takes every ounce of self-control in me to refrain from fucking her against that wall.

"Bet you have." I smirk. "How is your sister, anyway?"

Dana's arms cross over her chest, and she stares off to the left, scowling. "Fucked if I'd know."

It's been close to six years since I've seen her sister, and that's the answer I get? Sure doesn't ease the fucking guilt I have when I think about how I left that night.

"Sawyer, get the fuck out. Now!"

Fists pound the bedroom door as Mel points her black-lacquered nail towards the fire escape. Several angry bikers have a thirst for blood, and for good fuckin' reason.

A brother should never fuck the president's daughter. Especially after he's been specifically told to stay away.

But then, I never was one to follow rules . . .

"She left the club a year or so after you did. Daddy's been trying to find her the last few weeks—I guess 'cause of this shit—but he can't track her down."

"She left the club?" The girl I remember was equally as feisty as her little sister here, born and bred on leather and gas.

"Said she didn't want a part in it if she couldn't do it her way."

There you go. Makes more sense now. "Still doesn't explain why you're here."

"No." She scowls. "It doesn't."

"What shit's goin' down that has your old man lookin' for Mel?" Only a threat to the family would have that proud bastard admitting fault and running after his daughter.

"How would I know what's going down?" she shouts, throwing her hands up. "I don't get told that shit."

True—what did I expect? I eye the fit young thing as she stands penned between the wall and me. Trapped. It would be so easy to take her right here, right now. But for some sickening reason I can't understand, let alone recognize, I don't want to. I've never turned down an easy take before. What the fuck is going on?

You care . . .

Yeah, whatever asshole.

I beat a closed fist to my head and turn away. Since when do I care about other people? I stopped wasting time on that pointless exercise years ago. She's just a captive in my father's house, a toy for me to play with. I sure as fuck don't care how she feels about what I plan to do with her.

Do I?

revelations

"Ouch! You're hurting."

I yank the bitch along by her wrist, thundering toward my father's den. The last time I fucked one of Judas's daughters I damn near lost my manhood—literally. If I'm going to even consider sinking into this inked package, I need answers. And she does, too. Dana stumbles behind me, her fucking boots pounding on the marble floor as we cross the foyer.

"We're getting this shit squared up before I decide to fuck my way into another death sentence," I growl. "You want to know why you're here, and I want to know why you're here, so let's find out."

As I'd expected, my old man sits reclined in his leather chair, scotch in one hand, his ankle to his knee. I enter none-too-quietly with Dana, and stop in front of him. He ignores my presence, as he always does, and continues to watch some news report on the small flat-screen mounted in the top corner of the office.

The reporter describes the witness reports gathered after the discovery of three bodies in a house downtown. She matter-of-factly states the particulars: the time of discovery, the grizzly surroundings, the victims' connections to illegal activities, and the lack of suspects in the case.

My father smiles smugly, sipping on his scotch every so often. He looks so fucking pleased with himself as the reporter throws back to another man who begins to rattle off the list of suspicious murders that have occurred during the last three weeks. Still, my father doesn't look at me, speak to me, or so much as change his posture.

He doesn't respect you. Still thinks of you as a boy . . .

A cog skips on its rotation, my head rings with the sound of grinding gears, and the small tic at the corner of my eye makes an appearance. My palm lashes out, and the glass that occupied my father's hand seconds before now lies in a pile of shattered glass at the base of the wall, which drips with well-aged scotch.

He's out of the chair, his hands at my throat before I complete my next breath. Adrenalin floods my veins, and the muscles in my chest tense and pop as I thrust my arms inside of his. Pressing outward, I force his grip off of my throat, and his arms fling out wide.

"You insolent little bastard," he yells.

I steal a look at the girl, and laugh inside when I find her standing in the doorway, face as impassive as fucking ever. The lifestyle's done a fine fucking job of breaking her in to violence.

Turning back to my father, I ask, "What the fuck you plannin', old man?" I punctuate my question with a shove to his shoulder.

His arm sweeps behind his back and returns to me with a gun in his grasp. He presses the cool barrel under my jaw and sneers. "Touch me again, Son. See how it ends."

"You wouldn't fuckin' shoot me," I say, pushing onto the steel. "You need me, don't you?"

He re-holsters his weapon and steps away, chuckling. "Smart little shit when you want to be, aren't you?"

"Why are we here?" Dana asks, a small tremor in her words.

My father marches across the room to her, and takes a fistful of her hair. She winces as her head is bent to an unnatural angle, and he leads her across the room until she's brought within inches of my face.

"Why is the cunt talking to me, Sawyer?"

I stare coolly at him. "Because she has a mouth, you fuckin' retard."

He shunts her off to the side, and she crashes hip first into the side of a table. A pained cry escapes her lips and she crumples to the floor. My fists flex, and knuckles crack as my father resumes his position beside the chair.

"You kids these days, and your fucking smart mouths. They'll get you killed, you know," he announces loudly with his arms outstretched. I watch him move across the room toward a drink cabinet. He re-pours his scotch, and takes his seat. "You want to know why you're here? Because you two are part of my newest expansion. That's why."

Dana's brow furrows, and she pushes herself upright. Her eyes beg me to ask the question she can't without being manhandled again.

"Why us?" I say.

"Come on, Sawyer," my father replies with a chuckle. "You're a clever boy. You work it out."

I nod slowly, fully aware how this bastard works—all for his own benefit. "King's lot aren't going to just return your lost distribution to you, are they? You're going to blackmail him into running it, too."

He claps at my observation, slowly at first, but quickly gaining momentum. "Oh, bravo."

"What roles do we play, though?"

Dana nods beside me, agreeing with my question.

"Meet the new president and first lady of the Fallen Aces, southern," he says, eyes on the television and finger waving between us. "I need somebody I can manipulate in that role, and who better than you? You already have a history with them. It shouldn't be hard to convince your whore's dear old daddy to make you the VP. He should be getting his 'gift of persuasion' in about"—he checks his Tag Heuer watch— "one hour."

"What the fuck have you done?" I seethe.

"It was more what you did, boy. Tell me, she scream for you when you fucked her behind her daddy's back like she did for me when I took her fucking head off?"

A pained moan echoes around the room, and Dana falls to her knees beside me. "You fucking monster," she howls.

My father stands, and takes a grandiose bow. "Why, thank you, my dear."

She scrambles to her feet and lunges, but I catch the back of her shorts by the waist and haul her kicking and screaming into my hold. I get it, I really do. The thought of what Mel suffered in her final minutes has *me* ready to puke, but this isn't going to get us anywhere.

It never has—I've tried.

And failed . . .

"You're messed up if you think we'll play a part in this," I tell my father. "You're seriously fuckin' messed up."

"And you're kidding yourself if you think you have a choice, boy. Look around you. Whose house are you in? Who's in control here?"

Won't be for much longer if I have a say in it. I glare at the asshole and turn, with Dana still struggling to get free from my grasp. As I wrestle her toward the door, my father takes one last jab.

"Don't try and leave, Sawyer. The guards are instructed to shoot to kill."

No kidding. I'm struggling with the urge to let Dana go and see how much damage she can inflict on the guy—just for kicks.

Instead, I carry her against my chest, pressing her body into mine. She thrashes and sobs all the way to my room where I drop her onto the bed. Dana scrambles off and starts running for the hallway again, determined to have her revenge. I take after her, and manage to shoulder her into a wall before she reaches the foyer.

"This isn't going to help," I growl. "I get it, baby, I do. But chasing after blood when you're upset isn't smart."

"What the fuck is, then?" she asks. "He killed my sister. He fucking killed her," she wails.

"I know," I say pathetically, taking her weight as she collapses into my chest.

"It's not fair!"

There's nothing else I have for her. I'm not used to being the one who consoles people. What do I say when my father just murdered her sister, probably out of spite toward me? What can I say when, had the tables been reversed, I probably would have done the same? What the fuck can I say to that?

I slip an arm behind her knees, and lift her against my chest once more. The girl is falling to pieces under my touch and the best I can do is offer her support while she grieves, as bittersweet as that is when it comes from me. Her tears dry, but her breathing becomes desperate gulps for air as the pain wracks her body. She's distraught, and all I can do is lay her on the bed and stare.

Even my devil is taken aback as he silently watches on, intrigued. Neither of us have borne witness to this side of the pain before—we've always dealt it and then left. All I know is that there are no words for what she's going through, and there's nothing I can do to bring Mel back.

You killed her, you know . . .

No, she died because my father likes to fuck with people's emotions to get what he wants. And in a way, don't I, too? An acrid taste rises in my throat. I'm more like the bastard than I'd like to admit. I'm better at destroying people than fixing them. I hurt, not help.

But even so—even if I can't do a damn thing to make her feel better, I can do something else . . . I can help her get a fucked-up and brutal revenge.

I'm good at that.

disturbances

Dana lies on top of the comforter, occasional sobs shaking her body even in sleep. I sit in the large armchair beside the picture window and watch the moths dance around the gatehouse light. The night is still and quiet. No living thing strolls the grounds beside the guards: no birds, not so much as a rabbit. Every life form on this fucking planet knows better than to tread on the perfectly manicured lawns of my father—safety of darkness or not.

I stretch out in the seat, sliding down so I'm as close to horizontal as I can get. The room is stark of anything that was mine; white walls hold no art or posters and the furniture is new, replaced since I left. As I stare up at the ceiling, I note even the dents I'd caused with a ball, as a teenager, have been removed. If this is how he's scrubbed me from his life, his *living* son, then I can only imagine how little of my mother remains in the house.

Perhaps I'm literally all there is of her legacy. Although, with me here, how long will her memory last? If my old man kills me, he kills all that remains of her as well.

Ring-a-ring of roses, a pocket full of posies . . . we all fall down.

The night blends to dawn as I sit and think, unable to sleep. The noise in my head doesn't grant me much peace, and more often than not I give up trying to fight the din created by the devil in my head and just let him speak.

Kill the girl . . . create a diversion . . . but kill him before you go . . . leave his eyes till last so he can see you tear him apart . .
.

The things he tells me swirl in a cesspool of horror, blending into a gruesome plan for my father's torturous death.

I shift my gaze to the bed and watch Dana's sleeping form as her chest rises and falls. She's lying on her side, hands tucked beneath her head, and completely open and vulnerable.

Just like Ramona sleeps.

It pains me to see another woman so freely trusting of me. Why do they continue to do this? Is she the same as Ramona, thinking she can get inside this messed up fucking brain of mine and fix the short in the wiring?

Good luck with that . . .

I resume my observation of the moths as the lucid half of my mind drifts to Ramona. As crazy as I am, she's the only rational thought I ever fucking have. Her soft eyes while she fed me last night, and her gentle touch haunt me—the woman has infected me. Her constant concern for me was cute at first, but now it's fucking unsettling. I don't deserve her dedication, and yet she gives it anyway. I don't think what I feel for her is love, but I sure as fuck know it borders on manic possession. She's mine, nobody else's. My saint. My keeper. The mother of *my* child.

Mine.

And now, I have another woman in my bed who I feel the same sick possession for—the same need to hoard and guard as my own. I can't be sure what our connection is yet, but I sure as fuck know I don't want another man laying a hand on her either way.

Because she's my toy, and you can't have it . . .

Yeah, I even want to protect her from him—the fucker in my head who wants to make her bleed.

But if that's all my infatuation is, a fucked up need to make the woman mine and nobody else's, what is it? Obsession? It's not love. It's . . . I don't know. Fuck, how do I really know my infatuation isn't *based* on love? What have I got to compare to? I'm making broad assumptions based on what I know, which when it comes to women, isn't a lot.

Their bodies are these playgrounds that I frequent to get my thrills, but if I needed to understand how a woman's head worked, I'd be fucking lost. What goes on up there? Why is it they cry every time I tell them the honest truth? Why is it that a woman who wears her heart on her sleeve is the only fucking thing I'm going to miss now I'm home? Why do I always treat Ramona so shit, determined she'll wake up from her fucking daydream and leave me like she should?

She'll never leave you—you made sure of that . . .

My son—Mack.

The kid's so *pure*. His little mind hasn't been tainted by the demons that hide in the interactions he'll have as an adult. Everyone has a fucking agenda these days. Nobody is your friend. It pains me to think of the day he'll discover that.

If only I could preserve him, keep him so unjaded. But it'll never be. The boy will grow and he'll learn what hurt is. He'll learn what it is to be betrayed by not only the people you love and trust, but by *yourself.*

It's not betrayal, you fool; it's sabotage . . .

A shudder ripples my body, and I grit my teeth until it passes. What I'd do to know exactly what it was that changed me into *this.* What was it that made the happy kid grow into a lunatic? Okay, I had some traumatic things happen when I was young, but other people have that and they're not listening to conversations held by a devil camped out in the forefront of their mind. I'm fucking crackers—the whole motherfucking basket short of a picnic. I know this. Everyone else knows this. But knowing it and *understanding* it are two very different subjects.

When it comes to my insanity, I'm as lost as the next person on how to cure it.

And that is the reason why I've come to accept my madness—to let the devil from my shoulder move in to the dark chambers of my mind and set up shop. He's comfortable in there, controlling me, giving me ideas, and laughing as they fuck up everything about me. He's my ailment, but like an addict, I can't stomach a life without him. After all, he's the only friend I've got.

Without his voice in my mind, directing me toward my next train wreck, I'd have to do the most abhorred thing of all . . .

. . . I'd have to face the fact that I'm the only one responsible for ruining my life.

bonds

A sharp pain spreads up my shin as I wake, and I jolt upright in the chair. *When the fuck did I fall asleep?* Dana steps back from me and hesitates, weight on her back foot, ready to run.

"What the fuck?"

"Well, you wouldn't wake up when I shook you, so I kicked you in the leg." She eases her poised foot to the floor, and relaxes.

Kick her back . . .

"Thanks a fuckin' bunch," I growl.

"You want to eat? Some maid or something called Felicity was up here telling me breakfast is almost finished."

Breakfast. I forgot how orderly my father runs things. If it's almost over, then the morning has to be nearing eight o'clock. "Fuck him," I answer. "I'm not sitting at a table and playin' happy fuckin' families. I'll just raid the kitchen later."

She nods, and moves to stand by the window. "It's quite pretty here, eh?"

"Looks can be deceiving," I reply, swiveling in my seat to look at the gardener making passes on a ride-on mower. "I always thought of this place like a Venus fly-trap. It looks nice, but you get too close and *snap*, it fucking chews you up and spits you out."

"Sounds positively wonderful," she says dryly with a raised eyebrow. "Why did you come back, then?"

"Wasn't by choice. I was traded out."

Dana draws air between her teeth, making a hissing noise. "Ouch."

"Yeah, ouch. It was called for though. I was being an asshole." I let my mind wander to the past months, to all the bastard things I did to everyone at that club, most of all Mack. All the kid ever wanted was to spend some time with his old man, and what did I do? Shove him away.

Probably for the best. Wouldn't want the kid to turn out like his father now, would we? Might as well nip the fucked up behavior in the bud with my generation.

"I've been watching that gatehouse while you slept," Dana starts. "I think I've figured out their rotation habits. There's a weak spot where both of them are distracted for a bit."

"Don't bother," I tell her. "You wouldn't get far."

She looks to me, disbelieving. "How would you know?"

I stand, and brush shoulders with her at the window. A shiver skips across my flesh, and I take a step sideways to put space between us. "See that guy over there, in the corner to the right of the gatehouse?" She nods, watching the man walking towards us. "He's on a different rotation. When the guards swap over, he's over there, watching." I point to the top of the wall.

She follows my directive and her eyes grow wide when she spots the crow's nest partially obscured from our view by the small trees in the middle of the lawn. "Oh, right."

"Yeah, right. You wouldn't make it far before he took you out." I place a finger to her temple and make a soft 'boom' sound while I pull my pretend trigger.

"There's got to be a way," Dana insists.

"There is," I reply, grabbing her interest. "It's usually made from oak, and has six sides."

Her expression falls flat, and she shakes her head. "Yeah, not funny." Her gaze is fixed outdoors, watching the gardener as he empties the catcher on to the back of a pick-up on the driveway.

Grass isn't the only thing I've seen hauled out of that yard on the back of his truck.

That was your fault, you know . . .

Let's just say I never brought another girl home after that. Learnt pretty quick that the property was off-bounds to anyone my father hadn't invited in.

I head for the door, my stomach grumbling so loudly that anyone would think my throat had been cut. Hopefully Felicity left me a little something, as she used to when I was a kid. More often than not, I'd spend my mealtimes in the kitchen with her and the cook, listening and laughing as she recounted crazy stories about her family back in Venezuela. I could really go one of her breakfast bagels about now.

"Where you going?"

"I'm hungry," I answer simply.

Dana hurries from the window to where I stand, rubbing her thin arms. "Do you think Felicity could find me a jersey or something?"

I nod, and turn to hide my grin. "Yeah, sure. Come on."

•• • ••

"This is so fucking good," Dana moans between mouthfuls of apple and cinnamon oats. "I usually have Cocoa Pops or something like it."

"How the fuck do you keep that tidy body if you eat shit food?" I ask.

Her gaze finds mine, and I cringe. Made that a little obvious, didn't I?

"You two kids like a coffee?" Felicity asks, floating around the kitchen.

"Sure," I say, as Dana nods also.

The chef—a guy I haven't seen before—steps around Felicity to grab his coat from a hook inside the walk-in pantry. "I best be off now, Fifi. Anything you want from town?"

Felicity shakes her head, and gives the older man a pat on the elbow. "No, Cedric. I'll be fine."

Dana watches the two of them intently, and I swear I can almost read the thoughts tracking through her head. "I know what you're thinking, and no, they check his vehicle too."

She blows out an exasperated breath, and resumes spooning the last of her oats. There's no denying it; she's determined.

Felicity places our coffees before us on the counter with a jar of creamer and a small bowl of sugar. I take the spoon in the bowl and lump three full heaps into my black coffee.

"You like a bit of coffee with your sugar?"

A wry smile graces my lips and I add another spoonful, just for her. "I need sweetening." My devil cringes at our light exchange. I can't blame him—it's so unlike me.

Dana smirks in return and lumps a single spoonful into her drink before adding a dash of creamer. The spoon clinks around the inside of the cup, and her expression is forlorn. I give her a nudge, and when she doesn't respond, I kick her leg.

Payback.

"Hey!" she cries.

"Where'd you go?"

"Just thinking." She taps the spoon on the side of the cup, and then places it gently beside the sugar bowl, fussing until it's perfectly parallel.

"About?" I ask, following the question with a swig of Felicity's tar-like blend. Dana glares at me from the corner of her eyes, and I roll mine in response. "Apart from the obvious."

"Did he really cut her head off?"

I have no doubt. "Probably just said that to fuck with you."

"Yeah," she mumbles. "Probably." Her chest rises with a heavy breath. "It worked."

"Don't let him get to you. He's good at gettin' under your skin when you're not payin' attention."

She nods slowly, and pushes her breakfast bowl to the far side of the counter. Felicity scoops it up and proceeds to clean the residue off in the sink. Dana watches her with a twinge of guilt in her eye. "I didn't mean for her to think she had to take it."

"It's her job," I say, catching Felicity's eye and giving her a wink.

Dana and I continue to chat about the current situation

while we down our coffee. She changes the subject after a while and tells me a little about what Mel did after I left, and where some of the brothers thought she'd ended up. I gesture to Felicity for another brew, and listen to Dana while I wait as she recounts some of the hijinks her and Mel got up to as kids. The softer side of Judas she's showing in her stories is so at odds with the man I remember trying to slice me in two that I let loose a chuckle.

"What?" Dana asks. "I hadn't got to the funny bit yet."

"Nothin', babe. Nothin' at all." I could tell her, sure, but why ruin the fucking memories of her old man when it's only him and her brother left in the family?

Our light and relaxed meal is cut to an end by the fast approaching footsteps of my father. *Has to ruin everything.* I eyeball his shoes when he stops in the doorway, as if entering would put him on par with the hired help—a massive no-go in his books. "Lunch promptly at twelve, Sawyer."

"Only me?" I ask, avoiding looking him directly in the eye.

"Only you. I've got other plans for the bitch before she joins us." He shifts his gaze to Dana. "You will be expected with Felicity at quarter to twelve in the sitting room."

Dana doesn't so much as twitch. I decide to answer for her to save theatrics from the old man.

"She'll be there."

"Of course she will. Little cunt will get her nose cut off if she isn't."

Always with the threats. "Fuck off, Dad. You made your point."

Dana sits with her hands fiercely gripping her hot cup,

eyes downcast into the brown brew. My father grunts his discord, and promptly disappears. Gently, I reach over and pry her fingers from the black ceramic mug. The pads are red, and hot to the touch.

"Are you going to make it more than five fuckin' minutes with the guy?" I ask.

She shrugs, and takes a long swallow of her drink. "I don't have a choice here, do I?"

"Not really." The last of the coffee is sickly sweet. I grimace at the taste, and place the cup on the counter. "I need a shower before this fuckin' circus starts. You be all right here?"

Dana smirks, and finishes her burning second cup. She screws her face up as she forces the hot liquid down, and wipes her lips with the back of one hand. "No place I'd rather be."

accompany me

Freshly cleaned and shaven, I exit the bathroom to find Dana now sitting on my bed. Her eyes flick between my clothes tossed over the floor and the towel around my waist. Challenge lies in the dark green depths of her irises.

Keeping watch on her, I advance toward her position, and stop directly over my threads. She holds my gaze like a pro as I smirk, and drop the towel. The slightest crinkle at the corner of her eyes gives it all away. Her lips flatten into a firm line, and her throat bobs.

Boys and girls, come out to play . . .

"Did you need something?" I ask. "Thought you were going to hang out in the kitchen."

She sucks in a staggered breath, and finally looks away. "Realized I missed the company. I'm feeling kind of nervous."

"What happens, happens. You can't change the inevitable by worrying about it," I say, tugging my boxer-briefs on.

"Easy for you to say," she grumbles. "You're used to him. I'm not. I mean, if he can kill Mel, then what next? Me?"

"Or me." I settle on the bed beside her. "What changed, Dana?"

"What do you mean?"

"Why did your old man suddenly bring you into the club? He did everything to fuckin' keep you away from us rough fuckers while I was there."

She sighs, and fidgets. "Mel would get so mad with him not telling us what was going down. Her and him used to have real good arguments. She pulled his gun on him one time—it's kind of funny to look back on." She twitches a sad smile. "Anyway, after you she got real pissed about Daddy saying who she could and couldn't see. He even set her up with the club member he wanted her to marry. So, she stopped just saying she would, and left." Her fingers trace invisible lines on the bedding while she takes a moment to go somewhere else in her head. "I guess in a way he must have been worried I'd do the same, 'cause after Mel walked out, he started taking me in on weekends. Before long I was there after school, then before school, and after a while nobody paid mind to whether I came or went. I don't know if what Mel said made a difference, or if he was just scared of losing me so he kept me close. Either way, I got used to always being there, and they got used to having me around."

"You promised to anyone?" If Judas went as far as setting Mel up, then I wouldn't put it past the fucker to have Dana married off already.

"No. Nobody's got enough balls to try." She chuckles. "They all like their dicks intact."

An unpleasant tingle spreads through my groin thinking back on what Judas tried to do to me for having at his oldest daughter. Not a day I want to repeat. So why am I sitting here, wondering how his youngest daughter would feel wrapped around my cock?

Why don't you find out?

"You wish it were different?" I ask.

She peeks out at me from under her lashes. "Of course I wish it were different. The club is loaded with young, good-looking guys, and there I am, put in a corner and told not to touch anything. It hurts thinking none of them find me attractive enough to try. They don't even talk to me half the time."

"Baby, you're *very* attractive. I don't doubt that half those assholes are walkin' around with a wood in their leathers whenever you're there."

She giggles softly. "You don't have to be nice."

"Sayin' it how I see it."

Her teeth sink into her soft bottom lip, and she peers up at me with big doe eyes. I reach out to touch her face, but she recoils. "Don't."

"Don't what?" I say, edging closer.

She scuttles over the covers, and drops a leg off the edge of the mattress. "Don't touch me like that. It's not right."

"Come on. Can't we have a bit of fuckin' fun if we're going to be stuck here?"

"Fun? Are you fucking kidding me?"

I shake my head. "No. Dead serious, baby. I've seen you lookin' at me. Figured I'd show you just how attractive I think you are."

"Yeah," she snarls. "That's it—I was just looking."

"Like the view, though?" I smirk.

She tucks her leg back on the bed and shrugs. "Of course I like, you moron." Dana sighs, and her face softens. "I'm just not in the right headspace for that kind of thing right now."

"Babe," I say, exasperated. "You and me are stuck in this fuckin' house for God knows how long. Way I see it, we have a fuck-load of time to kill. So what better way, yeah?"

"Jesus," she shouts. "You're just like the rest of them—you all think with your dicks first."

"Excuse me for being a man," I growl, grabbing her ankle.

I try to haul her body under mine, but she lashes out, kicking and twisting. "I've heard about you," she yells. "People said you were fucking cold-hearted and crazy. I thought maybe they were wrong, but it turns out they knew best all along."

"If you know what I'm like," I grumble, "then why start somethin' you don't want?"

She connects a foot to my jaw, and I let go. "I didn't say I didn't ever want it, Sawyer. I just didn't think you'd be such an asshole about it."

"So what?" I ask. "I was goin' to be different for you, was I? Did you think you could change me—is that it? You were goin' to fix the broken guy?"

"No!"

"Then what the fuck did you expect by flirting with me?"

"That you wouldn't take advantage like this. That you'd just be you!" she shouts.

"Woman, this is fuckin' me!" I snatch hold of her leg, and drag her across the bed. All this fighting has me raring to go, and if I don't get a warm hole to sink into in the next minute, my father's going to be short a hostage.

She kicks with her free foot, and rips at my hair with her fingers. I wince at the sharp pricks across my scalp, and fight to get her shorts off.

"This is not you, Sawyer. This is not who you are!"

She's wrong—so fucking wrong. This vile act is everything I am. I've never been anyone else. "Hold still, or I'm going to hurt you."

"Then fucking hurt me, you coward." Her palm connects with my cheek. "You're already acting like your fucking father, so have at me. Hurt me, Sawyer. Be your old man."

Her body bounces on the bed with the force I use to push her away. "I am not my old man, bitch. You fuckin' take that shit back."

"You're everything like your old man," she seethes. "At least, you act like you are. Go take a long, hard look in the mirror, and when you find the real man under all this bullshit, you let me know." She scrambles off the bed, and straightens her shorts over her legs. "I'm fucking out of here."

I sit back on my heels and watch her go, then look down at the hands that mere seconds before had her pinned to the bed against her will. She was right—my father would do that. He'd probably get off on the struggle like me, too, because we're of the same blood. I can't escape him.

Whatever I do, wherever I go, he's always going to be with me. Just like the devil in my head.

The devil in my head . . .

Fuck. He *is* the devil in my head.

canapés and cocaine

The enormous dining table is covered with an array of savory, sweet, and fruity offerings. I run my eye over the amount of food there is for the two of us, and lift my gaze to my father at the far end.

"Bit much, don't you think? Or are your new family going to meet the long-lost son?"

He chuckles, sardonically. "Don't be ridiculous. They're staying at our holiday house this week."

"Nice. Get the family out of reach of your crazy kid, huh?"

"Don't flatter yourself," he bites, glaring. "I've got other things I'd rather they weren't involved in."

"Must be hard, juggling your shady dealings with a wife and kid."

He grins, and my skin crawls. "Is it?"

Touché, you old bastard.

The hammering of steel on wood echoes outside the room, and is quickly followed by the hurried footsteps of Felicity across the entrance.

My father shifts his gaze to the dining room doorway, and places his laced fingers on the table before him. "Good. Our visitor is here." The squeak of leather and echo of heavy boots heads our way. "I believe you know each other."

My gaze moves to the doorway also, and the hulk of a man who enters has my balls shrinking inside my body. *Shit.*

I stand on shaky legs to greet one of the few men who still has the ability to instill fear in me—Judas. Dana's father, the president of the Fallen Aces southern chapter, eyes me slowly from head to toe, and then splits his lips into an evil gold-toothed grin. "Sawyer. What a nice fucking surprise."

I laugh awkwardly, and extend my hand. "Yeah. It is." Thank fuck he has no idea what I just tried to do to his daughter, otherwise he'd be doing a fuck-load more than shaking my hand.

My father eyes our bone-crushing shake with sick interest, and nods to Judas in acknowledgement. The big guy takes a seat at the side of the rectangular table, and leans forward to place both elbows on the tabletop. My palms slip over the wooden surface, and I bury them under the table, wiping furiously over the legs of my jeans.

The last time I saw this giant I'd been running in the opposite direction with only a T-shirt covering my body, blood running in thick streaks down my legs. I let loose an involuntary shiver, and concentrate on the now rather than reliving that horrid memory.

"You've grown up a bit," Judas says to me. "But I hear you're just as much of a fucking troublemaker as you were back then."

Felicity enters the room and pours a fresh coffee for my father. She passes Judas as he waves her off, and heads towards me. I nod, and watch her as she fills my mug with inky-black sustenance. Her dark hair has grayed slightly since I was last home, and there are three times as many laugh lines around her eyes, but the short woman is otherwise just as I remember her. She gives me a gentle pat on the forearm and then leaves, allowing my father to carry on the conversation.

"Tell me the story again, Sawyer," my father taunts. "Why was it you transferred between chapters?"

My sight fixes on the array of cutlery set out beside my plate: two forks, two spoons, three knives, and something I wouldn't even know what to do with.

You could stab him now . . . get it done . . .

I rub the heel of my hands into my eyes, and grumble, "I think you know why." My fading unease is fast being replaced by anger.

"But I want to hear it from you," my old man prods.

Judas chuckles and I suppress the urge to carry out a lunch edition of the *Texas Chainsaw Massacre.* My ears burn and the devil jumps up and down in his seat, screaming at me to do something. I can't focus my vision, and the blood coursing my veins leaves a painful roar deep in my ears.

"I don't think he wants to speak," Judas says. "Never did do as he was fucking told."

"Why am I here?" I explode, massaging my temples. "Why am I even a part of this fuckin' meeting?"

"You are here," my father bellows, pushing out from his seat to lean both hands on the table, "so you can bloody well rectify some of the damage you've done."

"To who?" I holler. "What does it fuckin' matter? I screw up, I do crazy shit, and I fuck people over, because . . . well, because I'm fucking nuts, Dad! I'm certifiably crazy, and you're the fucker who made me that way!"

The two men at the table laugh mercilessly at me. The pitch of their humor rings in my ears, and swirls about me. My father slaps the surface beside his plate, and clears his throat, commanding Judas's attention.

"Let him be for now," he says with a smile.

"Well then, Carlos," Judas prompts. "What's the news you have for me on the fuckin' bastard that took Dana, and messed up my Mel? You said you know who cut my baby's head off. I want a name so I can get my youngest daughter back and then fuck the mongrel over personally for taking my girl."

I cringe, knowing what's coming next.

"I need a little help explaining the story behind it, so let me just call on one more person, yes?"

Judas eyes him carefully, but opts to nod. *Clever man.*

My father leans back and claps his hands. Felicity appears through the door, and stands with her fingers clasped at her front. "Bring us our other guest, would you?"

She nods, and leaves, as my blood runs cold. My head pounds, and the devil at the wheel laughs hysterically. Nervous minutes pass as Judas and my father eat the fare before us. I stare at a slice of mango, unable to stomach the concept of putting it in my mouth, let alone trying. I'm sick to the core, fighting the urge to leave the room.

You had this coming . . .

Dana is led into the room, and positioned at the head of the table beside my father. Her eyes are a little red, and still puffy from our argument. Her hair is damp from a shower. I feel her gaze bore into me, but I can't bring myself to meet her line of sight.

I screw my eyes shut and prop my elbows on the table, covering my ears with my arms, ready for the onslaught. Even so, Judas's voice tears through my pathetic attempt at denial.

"What the motherfucking hell, Carlos?"

The scrape of a chair rouses my interest, as does the immediate cock of a gun that follows.

"Sit the fuck down, Judas."

The massive man drops into the seat, resigned, with my father's gun trained on his head. His face is pale, almost matching his gray beard. But most interesting of all, he chooses to watch Dana, *not* my father. If somebody had a gun on me, I'd be watching them, not the hostage—even if it were my kid.

"You said you'd find her," Judas whines with the voice of a broken man.

"Ta-da!" my father proclaims. "Found her."

"Daddy," she consoles him quietly. "It's okay." My heart shatters.

"Sugar," Judas replies. "Just hold tight."

My father snickers at the end of the table, highly amused by his set-up. It's mind-boggling how in the space of a half hour I can go from being terrified of Judas, to looking at him with compassion. The big guy is freaking out, and if that were my daughter, I would be too.

Her eyes are large as she watches her father unravel, and I marvel at how stunning she looks, even in distress. I can understand why he kept her out of the club life when she was younger—otherwise *this* kind of shit would have happened sooner.

"What do you want, then?" Judas asks, back into business mode.

My father runs a confident finger over the tabletop, and smiles. "Your club."

Judas splutters. "Excuse me?"

"I want you to hand the club over to Sawyer—make him vice president so that he'll become your successor."

"I can't do that without a vote. It's not how we do things."

My father stands, walking behind Dana. She stiffens as he runs a hand over her shoulder, down her back, and cups her ass. "I can't let her go without getting something in return. It's not how *I* do things."

Judas's gaze narrows, and my skin burns with the rage my father creates inside of me. I've hated the man since I was born, I'm sure of it. My mouth opens to protest, but the devil inside of me clamps his fingers around my windpipe, choking any sound.

Just wait it out. You're getting a club out of this . . .

My head's into the idea, my sick desires feeding off the thought of a bunch of people at my whim, but way in the back row, smothered by the guilt of every murder, rape and beating I've committed is my conscience, screaming for release.

"I hand the club to the kid, and then what? You just hand me Dana? I don't see you letting her go that easy."

Her gaze finds mine, and we hold our connection while our fathers bicker and barter. She's amazingly calm throughout the whole thing. It's impressive and a little unnerving.

"If I return having made your boy VP, why the fuck would you then let us walk out of here," Judas snaps, "you'll shoot us before we get to the fuckin' gate."

"Maybe." My father shrugs, toying with strands of Dana's hair.

Seeing his fingers on her, near her, anywhere within a ten-foot radius has me simmering to a boil. If he keeps it up, I'm liable to flip the fucking huge table just to get to them.

"I want assurances of her safety," Judas demands.

My father raises his eyebrow. "And not yours?"

He shakes his head, resigned. "I know you too well, Carlos. You'd never offer that much. Just spare my daughter."

The decision pains my father, his face bunched as he paces to the far side of the room. "No."

"Why the fuck not?" Judas screams. "What kind of fuckin' sick asshole are you? You think your boy is the one who's lost his head," he thunders. "It's you, you sick fuck."

"Why spare her?" my father asks. "She's only here to give you a nudge in the right direction. You refuse to do this, to vote Sawyer in, and I'll take my time hurting her nice and slow. Nothing too severe—just enough to make her cry while she wonders what's coming next" He chuckles, and shakes his head. "What the fuck—let's start now."

My old man spins around, and the gun in his hand lifts. Judas moves toward Dana with lightning speed for such a big guy, but it's not enough. I'm sliding across the table as the bullet grazes her shoulder, sending her reeling into the wall behind her. She crumples to the floor with a cry, clutching her injured arm.

Judas and I scramble to Dana's side as the crazy, unhinged

laughter of the man who gave me this fucked up life echoes around us. She glances between the two of us kneeling before her, and then reaches her hands between us to place them on our shoulders and push outward. I topple to the side as another bullet whistles between her and I, lodging in the plaster of the wall behind her.

Judas tugs her hand, scrambling across the floor toward the door. My father's shoes slam the marble as he rushes around the table for a clear shot. Reaching out, I tackle him to the ground; the gun goes off again beside my head in the struggle, and a deafening white noise fills my ear. I struggle with him through the drone, watching his mouth move as he yells at me, and every strike of my fist against his flesh lands in relative silence.

Equally matched, we both receive the same amount of damage. The distinct warmth of blood trails from my nose, and a dull throb in the side of my eye tells me I'm going to have one hell of a shiner. My father doesn't fare a lot better, with a split lip and bruising already forming on his jaw and neck. He throws an elbow my way, and I lean to the left to avoid the blow.

The tinnitus from the gun blast eases, and my father's muted swearing starts to trickle in through the racket. As I lay another hit into his cheek, another sound mixes with the garbled words spilling from his lips.

Crying.

I push my father away, and swing my foot around to kick the gun out of his reach. He rolls to his front to stand and retrieve it, but a quick heel to his wrist has him writhing and wailing like a little girl on the floor.

The crying comes through loud and clear as the ringing stops, and I spin around to find Dana on the floor, cradling Judas's head in her lap. Blood coats her shorts, dripping down her legs from the steady stream pumping over her hand. She has her palm pressed firmly into his neck, just shy of the jugular. She's sobbing, bargaining with God to take her instead.

"Look what you've gone and made me do," my father complains. "Everything, Sawyer—everything you come near turns into a great big fucking mess."

I stand, and stare at the carnage before me.

Even in this desolate hour, at the pivotal moment when she's lost her father's life, Dana's still beautiful. And I'm still sick for thinking so.

"Do something," she screams. "Help him!"

I take one look at Judas, and shake my head. His eyes are vacant, cloudy. The amount of blood over the floor tells me he's beyond saving. The human body can only lose so much. "He's gone," I whisper. I kneel down before her, listening to my father groan from his position on the floor, and duck my chin to my chest. "I'm sorry."

She wails, a broken, defeated howl cracking from her throat. I reach out to comfort her, but she flips. Her small hands form fists, and she beats me as hard as she can, covering me with her father's blood.

"It's your fault. It's all your fault," she yells.

My father's grunts of pain turn to laughter, and the sequences in my head skew.

Just kill him . . .

I push to my feet, fully intending to pick up that gun and

blow the last bullets into his skull, yet find myself facing the business end of the barrel. His finger tenses, depressing the trigger. My eyes are screwed shut, and I'm ready to feel the bite of my maker.

Click.

"Ah, fuck it." He laughs hysterically at me, shaking the expended gun in his hand. "I wasted a few bullets already on a stupid whore who decided to go through my wallet last night." The sick bastard smiles at the weapon, clearly reminiscing. "Besides," he says with a sigh, "it would have screwed things up a little if you were dead, so probably for the best that I didn't kill you. I really need to get this impulsiveness under control . . ." he trails off.

My heart is drumming a heavy beat in my ears, my head aching. My old man looks over my shoulder at where Dana sits, sobbing with Judas's lifeless body draped over her legs. Aside from her, all I can hear in this fucking room is my breath as it pulls into my lungs in short, heavy bursts.

He really tried to kill me.

The devil laughs. *Did you think he was bluffing . . .?*

"You should see all your faces," my father exclaims. "Everyone hold still." He pulls his phone from the pocket of his slacks, and snaps a picture of our stunned scene.

My jaw tics, and a twitch breaks into a rapid beat beside my nose. My fists are tight, my frown firm, and I'm ready to find out just how long it takes to kill a man with my bare hands when Dana calls my name.

"Sawyer . . . let him go."

Why? "Are you thinkin' straight?" I growl, spinning to face her.

"Clearly not," she hisses. "In case you haven't fucking noticed, I'm holding on to my dead father." Her voice grows with her anger. "He's the second member of my family killed by your fucking father this week, so excuse me if I want to fucking have a break from this fucking insanity!"

I spin back to the bastard in question before my urge to shut Dana up overwhelms me. "What the fuck you gonna do now, old man?" I ask. "He was your ticket to gettin' me in, so looks like your plan's a little on the fucked up side, huh?"

"I'll think of something," he retorts, his face screwed up as he eyes the blood splattered about the room. "Just get the fuck out of here. I need to get this cleaned up before your fucking blood stains my furnishings."

"I'm not going anywhere," Dana says firmly. "You are *not* taking my father from me."

"Bitch, what exactly do you plan on doing with his corpse?" my father asks her. "You have a way of disposing of it yourself that I'm not aware of? Because if you do, I'm all ears for new ideas."

She wriggles out from underneath Judas's head and shoulders, and steps over the body as she advances towards where my father stands. "You will not dispose of him like the fucking garbage, you hear me?" She reaches him, and starts to beat his chest and head with her small fists. He simply stands and takes it. "You fucking killed him, and now you want me to let you take his body away to be chopped and burned?"

"Fed to pigs, actually," my father retorts, dodging a blow. "We're organic here."

Dana loses what's left of her control. Her words pour out

in a jumbled mess. She screams with such force her voice is reduced to a husky croak and the tears which stream across her face suck into her mouth with each ragged breath. She coughs, and chokes, still trying to scream away her anger, her grief and her loss of hope. Yet the message is wasted, wasted on a man who couldn't care less what he's done to her world.

Normally, that man would be me, and the realization hits me full force as I stand and watch this crazy little woman unleash her fury on my father. Until this point, I'd always seen myself as reckless, without care, and for the most part crazy. Anything and everything I did was to prove to the graying man before me that I could be *better*. But am I? Watching her despair course through her body, her anger fuel her strikes, gives me such a new perspective on all of this. How many times have *I* been that guy, being pummeled for being such a monster, so thoughtless and so *heartless*? How many times has it been me who stood impassive throughout the onslaught, letting the broken person before me—the person *I* broke—run their course . . . and then just walked away from it all?

I'm just like him. I'm as fucking heartless as my father.

It can't continue.

I reach out and take a hold of her wrist as she rears her arm back for another blow. Dana starts, and turns her confused expression toward me. "What are you doing?" she wails.

"Stopping the cycle," I say, and drag her kicking and clawing from the room.

My father stands rooted to the spot as we leave. I catch a

glimpse of him as we round the door, turning for his liquor stand. Many a time before I've seen him do the same—he creates carnage, takes a life, and then drinks himself into a stupor. The alcohol is a duster for his slate. It's how he forgets, not that I honestly believe it would worry the fucking man if he didn't.

Dana sobs quietly, now following a few steps behind me of her own accord as we near my room. I step inside, wait for her to pass and then shut the door. She retreats to the chair by the window, curling herself into a ball within its arms. I cross the room and stand on the opposite side of the window, leaning a shoulder into the wall. She reaches up, fidgets with her hair, and then pulls it across her face so I can't see her red and puffy eyes.

"How's your shoulder?" I ask.

She gingerly touches her bloody sleeve, and hisses. "Sore, but nothing serious."

"As much as I hate to admit it," I say, "he was right. We had no way to get your father's body out of here and into a proper fuckin' burial."

"He tried to kill *me* first," she murmurs. "It was supposed to be me."

"Yeah? And then what? Your father would have lost two of his kids? A parent's not meant to bury a child, you know."

"And a child isn't supposed to try and stop the life literally pouring out of their parent, either."

Touché.

"What now, then?" I ask her. "You need some time to yourself? Or you want me to stick around?"

"Time to myself would be appreciated," she says, her hair

still obscuring her face.

"Guess I'll just leave you to it then." I hesitate, waiting for a retraction, but she doesn't reply.

Taking my boots with me, I make my way to the foyer, intending to head outdoors for some fresh air. Fred, one of the grounds men, wheels a barrow out of the dining room—a crude canvas sheet has been thrown over Judas's body. Bowing my head, I give some respect as the guy passes by. The goliath may have been an asshole, but he was one out of expectation. Nice guys don't last long in our world. People like Judas had to be rough and intimidating or risk being walked over. People like my father . . . well, they're just assholes by choice.

Fred crosses through the front doors and sets the barrow down to tuck one of Judas's hands back within the tub. He glances at the front steps, and sighs.

"You need a hand, Fred?" I tug my boots on as he answers.

"That would be grand, Sawyer."

Between the two of us, we manage to lift the barrow and carry it to the bottom—a lot easier than Fred having to keep it balanced while he walked down the steps backwards. I set the front end down on the driveway, and take a step back as Fred wheels the body away. Glancing up, I catch sight of Dana still in the chair, still watching.

The afternoon sun has dimmed and dark clouds line the horizon. With a lack of extra clothing to use should I get wet, I decide to skip the walk outdoors and settle for a stroll through the house. It's been an age since I've set foot in some of the rooms—especially those where my mother spent most of her time. Having just witnessed a family torn to shreds, I'm feeling now is about as good a time as any to rip open some old wounds, and reminisce.

I'm in the foyer, finishing up taking my heavy boots off again when the glossy black shoes of my father stop in my line of sight. "Need something?" I ask.

"Turns out the situation isn't quite as dire as we'd expected," he says, chipper. "You want to guess who the current VP is?"

"Couldn't care less," I mutter, straightening up.

"Judas's only son, and Dana's brother—Hooch. Seems the guy is quite popular, so I have no doubt that come tomorrow, we'll have a new president to be negotiating with."

"And then this sick merry-go-round starts again."

"Exactly." My old man shunts his hands in his pockets, proud and smug as fuck of his 'good fortune.'

"What if I want no part in this?" I seethe. "What if I tell you to go fuck yourself and your plans for expansion? I don't even know what made you think I'd agree to help you in the first place."

My father pulls his phone from his pocket, and ignores me while he runs his thumb over the screen. "I believe I have the perfect reason why you'd help me." He turns the phone around and shows me a picture of Ramona and Mack walking from her car to the front door of the house they're staying at. I look at the date on the top of the display and draw blood from biting the side of my tongue so hard.

Yesterday.

"You followed us yesterday, before the meet?"

My father rolls his eyes as he pockets the phone. "Of course. What do you take me for? Stupid? I had to know where you all were in case everyone decided to stage a no-show."

"So you knew I was at that house?"

"The whole time," he says, grinning maliciously.

"Why didn't you just fuckin' take me then? Why the whole 'meet' thing?"

He glares at me in a *'are you really so stupid'* sort of way.

"Right," I drag out. "I'm real useful for you, huh?"

"Right time, right place, Sawyer. That is all."

If I thought it was bad enough when he openly told me how he intended on using me for his expansion plans, then fuck did I have another thing coming. Knowing now that the asshole had used me *without* my knowledge to get my club to regain his lost distribution? *Fucker.*

The light is fast dimming before the rain, and long shadows stretch across the open foyer as I shake my head and turn away. I need time alone, time to fucking unwind and regroup. This past day has been a complete and utter mind-fuck. So many things that I thought I knew. So many things that I thought I had figured out about where I'm at in my life—gone. Everything I thought I knew about myself is fucking whistling away with the wind, and all I can do is stand and stare while my life unravels before me.

Some guy I am, huh? Parading around the country thinking I'm fuckin' ten-foot tall and bulletproof, all while my old man is quietly fucking me over from his comfy leather office chair, playing with my life like it's a motherfucking chess piece.

"What did you think, Sawyer?" he asks with a chuckle. "Did you really think that you could leave it all behind, and simply walk away? Were you that fucking delusional that you really believed you *ever* left my control?"

"You hated the fact I joined the Angels," I remind him, stepping forward. "You fucking despised it."

"Did I?" he asks, raising an eyebrow.

Motherfucker. How much more of this can I take before my head falls apart? "You've been planning this from all the way back then?" I croak.

"I'd be as crazy as you are not to. The Fallen Aces have one of the most widespread networks throughout this country. So what if they only have three chapters? It's the people they know, the *reach* they have that I need."

"Why do it this way? Why not work on King? Why not wait for me to get to the top on my own?" The depth of my father's deception has been revealed, and yet, I'm still whining about not being able to 'do it on my own'. *Fucking sad, little man.*

He laughs, shaking his head. "Boy, you were never going to make it through the ranks of either chapter on your own. You're a walking disaster—your own worst enemy."

My pulse beats heavy in my temples as I stare at him. How could he use me so . . . coldly? I'm a business transaction, an asset. I'm nothing more than a moveable piece of equipment, depreciating on his balance sheet. I'm no more of a living, breathing person to my father than the ostentatious marble statue of David in the center of his fucking driveway is.

I have to get away from him—from the reminder that everything I've done since I escaped this house has been in vain.

I never escaped—I simply expanded my enclosure.

reminiscing

The entire north wing of the house is shrouded in darkness, and the chill in the air tells me it's been a while since anybody has frequented this part of the home.

Scrap that.

A *home* would be a place where somebody feels *welcome*, loved, and at the very least encouraged. A home is the kind of place you want to return to after a hard day sloughing in the fucking pits for a dollar. Not this sterile trench of lies. These halls have absorbed twice as much negative energy as positive in the time I've spent here. The horror they could speak of would set a chill in the bones of the most hardened psychopath. Sure as fuck gives me the heebie-jeebies.

I shoulder my way through the heavy wooden doors that separate the living rooms at this end of the house from the bedrooms. Dust lines the window sills in banks of gray snow, and the lamp and table setting that fills the large space at the end of the hallway has been covered in a cloth. My spine tingles, and on a whim, I spin around to check behind me, laughing when I find nothing there but my own shadow.

Just your ghosts . . .

Pondering if my craziness is hereditary, I carry on the way I was originally headed and reach the dark timber doors at the end of the hall. My warm hand weighs down on the cold latch, and the door eases open with the grace of the lady who once inhabited this room—my mother.

All of her possessions have been removed, and even the furniture is pushed to one side, upturned, and covered in cloths. I draw a deep breath and make my way to the middle of the room where I sink to the mosaic centerpiece on the otherwise stark white tiled floor. Tucking my knees up inside of my arms, I let the heavy air in my lungs go and stare at the hazy images that replay in the room as if from a faded movie. My chest hums with the same rage I'm determined to use when I finally kill my father for what he did.

"No! I swear I won't say a thing. I'm sorry, I'm so sorry . . . just no . . ." My mother's voice recedes into a guttural moan as she continues to plead.

"Enough!"

My limbs shake, and I cower under the bed as my father slaps my mother over and over. Her head reels from the impact, and blood trickles down her chin in a delicate stream of crimson. I choke back a sob, knowing he'll find me if I make a noise. It's not supposed to be like this . . .

Spit flies from my father's lips as he yells at her. "Who was he, Sherry? A detective? An undercover? Your fucking lover?"

"I'm not sure," my mother cries, lifting her hands to fend off the blows she knows will come. "I've never seen him before today."

"What did he promise you, sweetheart? What did he

fucking say he'd do for you that I can't?"

My heart thumps heavily into the unforgiving marble floor beneath me, my skin slick with sweat. I've never seen him this angry. I've never seen him so mad at my mother. They've argued, fought, and always made up.

But this is so wrong.

My hands slam over my ears. I don't want to hear any more. I can't stomach his anger, his hate. I don't want to—

The thud as my mother's body hits the floor breaks through my feeble defenses. I lie in shock, in a trance, trying to breathe as I stare into the warm brown eyes of the woman who threw down her life to protect me, watching as they fade into a dull grey.

My mother is gone. I know because I have the blood splatter on my face to prove it.

More than twenty years have passed, and yet my chest still hurts, aching under the strain I place on myself while I do my best not to break down. I'm taken back to that night, to the moment when I realized just how monstrous my father truly was as her slit throat pulsed blood over the floor and under my small hands. I was a child, too young to defend her, but old enough to understand what she was trying to do, and what she'd lost her life lying about.

My old man had connections back then who'd helped him become the powerhouse he is today, a bunch of men in his pocket and at his disposal—ex-colleagues from his days working as a detective for the precinct, and a few judges tossed in for good measure. All the evidence in the world couldn't convict him for what he did—it still can't. He's untouchable.

My father the drug lord. My father the ex-cop. My father the wife murderer.

Two days was all we needed. Two more days and my mother would have found us a way to be relocated to a safe house, to escape the spiral into Hell she could see happening. She married him as a beautiful, naïve bride who wanted nothing more than to support her husband in his job serving the community, and she died a frightened woman who tried until her dying breath to give her child an exit from the corrupt man she no longer loved.

A modern day tragedy. My fucking tragedy.

The same day my head broke, and my brain lost the ability to deal with the world about me.

I tuck my face into my knees, and count through my breaths until the distress eases. The devil in my head runs his bony fingers over the horrific images as they fade from my mind's eye, nostalgic for completely the opposite reason. It was, after all, the day he was born. I'm on my twentieth breath, and holding the count when a the thud of the door shutting brings my head up in an instant.

Those transfixing green eyes watch me with a mixture of curiosity and concern as Dana crosses the room and kneels beside me.

"How did you find me?" I ask, running the heels of my hands quickly over my face. She doesn't need to see how weak I can be, how much of a fucking pussy I really am.

"I heard you argue with . . . *him*. I followed you."

Guess I wasn't imagining things in the hall, then.

I turn my face away, ashamed of what I am reduced to in

this room painful memories—my safe place. Dana wriggles closer and sits quietly beside me in the dark. She doesn't try once to touch me or console me. There are no wasted words of sympathy or fake sentiments. She just . . . sits there. Only our breathing punctures the otherwise silent night as I come to realize I'm falling hard and fast for this girl.

"I'm sorry for what I did," I say. "I wasn't thinkin' right."

"There he is," she says, giving me a nudge with her shoulder. "There's the nice guy I knew was in there."

"I wouldn't call me a nice guy," I reply sternly. "Don't go gettin' yourself confused there, sweetheart."

"Just you let me be the judge," she says with a chuckle. Silence stretches between us before she speaks again. "You said we'll never leave," she whispers, "but I think you're wrong."

Wrong—isn't that all I am of late? I'd love to be wrong on this one, too, but I'm certain there's no chance I could be. It's just . . . impossible. The place is heavily guarded, monitored and controlled. What can we do? We don't have any fucking weapons. Not even a slight advantage.

She watches me shake my head and asks, "What?"

"It's just," I say with a chuckle, "I thought I was crazy, but you've just taken the trophy, babe. There's just no fuckin' chance in hell that we'd make it more than twenty feet from the gate. Between the house and the road are at least two guys who spend their spare time layin' bets on who can hit nothing but the bull's eye at target practice."

Her fingers find my hand, and she slips the slender digits between mine. I meet her firm stare, and marvel at how alive her irises are, even in the dark. "I'll find a way," she says. "I'll find how we can get out of here."

"Why not just run on your own?" I ask, turning my body towards hers. "One person's got more chance at slippin' through the cracks, if you find any, than two. You very clearly pointed out how much of an asshole I am, just like my old man, so why bother to save me?"

She ducks her chin, and frowns. "I know I said that, but I was wrong. I heard the things he said to you, and it made me realize how narrow-minded I'd been." She gives my hand a squeeze and then lets go. "You never wanted any part in this, and I was wrong to blame you for it. It's him, all him, not you."

"You could save yourself," I stress. "Use me as a distraction. Fuck, I'll go get myself shot if it gives you enough of a head start. Forget about me, babe. I've blown my chances at a good life. Just work out how to get yourself out of this fuckin' shithole."

She shakes her head as a lone tear slides to the corner of her down-turned mouth. "I don't want to forget you. Why the fuck would I do that? You've been nothing but kind to me since we were dumped in this hell. Maybe it's not a lot to you, but it's something to me. You could have ignored me out there on the driveway; left me with your father, or turned a blind eye. But you didn't. For whatever fucking reason, you picked me up and you kept me safe. There's no reason I can think of that makes it okay to repay such a favor with selfishness."

"Every fucked up thing I've done is enough of a reason," I say quietly. Not to mention my initial intention was anything but 'keeping her safe'. "Every single fuckin' sin in my life is a reason why you have every right to be selfish."

"No, it's not. And you know why?" she says. "Because you never did any of that to me."

Why does she keep doing this to me—tearing my heart apart and causing this fucking pain in my chest?

My hands find her face, and I pull her head to mine. "What you just said right then proves you're ten times the person I am. You deserve to get out of here and to live your life so much more than I do, Dana. If I leave this fuckin' place, I'm only going to hurt people again." I close my eyes, and lean my forehead to hers. "I'm so fuckin' tired of hurtin' people."

"Then don't."

"It's not that simple," I whisper. "I don't know how to do anything else."

"You do," she counters. "Let me prove you can."

I open my eyes, and my lungs seize as I stare into those emerald gems. Dana shuffles her knees closer, until they touch mine. Her breathing quickens, and her hands gently touch my thighs at first, inching their way up my legs toward the part of me that is most keen to see what she has planned. All the while, her hypnotizing gaze holds mine.

She leans slowly forward and then hesitates just shy of my face; her quickening breaths tickle my mouth. For a moment she looks as if she'll say something—an admission maybe, but the thought flees from my mind as her soft lips press on top of mine. I freeze at her touch, ever so slightly, but it's enough for me to know and my panic sets in. I've never *wanted* a girl to just kiss me, nothing more, like I do now . . . and it's fucking unsettling. When the hell did I start to *feel* things for people like this? When did I start giving a shit how a girl chooses to kiss me?

She pulls back and simply stares, astonished. "I . . . I just . . ."

Before she can say another pointless word, I close the gap again and kiss her properly. My lips seal over her bottom one and I give it a little pull. She lets out a small moan, and mirrors the action before breaking the connection and sitting back on her heels. Her fingers graze her swollen lips, and she cracks a small smile. Those green pools light up as she gives a small chuckle.

"You okay?" I ask.

She nods, and her smile grows.

I trail my hands over her shoulders and down her sides until I reach the hem of her T-shirt. Taking hold of the torn edge, I tug upward, urging her to lift her arms. She obliges, and I slip the ratty fabric over her head. Her breasts sit round and high on her chest, and trepidation races through my veins at how fucking young she really is. She was a kid, kept away from the clubhouse when I was a part of Judas's crew. I never stopped to think exactly *how much* of a kid.

"How old are you?" I ask.

She leans back on her heels, and crosses her arms over her bare breasts. "Nineteen."

You know she is . . . don't ask . . . just take it . . . enjoy it, you fool . . .

I close my eyes and mentally place a gag in the fucker's mouth. "Have you had sex before?" The devil slaps a hand to his face.

Dana blushes and averts her gaze.

I shake my head, slowly at first, and then start to backtrack across the floor. I can't take that from her—not when this family has taken so much from her already.

She scrambles after me, and takes a hold of my T-shirt as I retreat. "No, Sawyer. Don't push me away."

"You shouldn't give me that," I say, trying to peel her hands from my clothing.

She lunges her hips forwards, and quickly wraps her legs about my waist. I place both hands on her stomach, and attempt to push her off. "You don't get it," I try to explain. "It should be with somebody special. Not me. Never me."

"I choose you," she says defiantly. "You *are* special to me."

My hands drop to my sides, defeated. "You were fuckin' kidnapped and brought here as a bribe," I explain. "How can you trust what you're feeling?"

Her face charges a storm, and she finally scrambles off me. I watch her beautiful eyes turn all shades as she works through the emotions. "I'm not stupid, you know. I'm young, but I'm not fucking stupid."

"Your head is playing tricks on you," I say, distressed to feel tears on my face. "You're tricking yourself into wanting me because I'm the only one who's shown you kindness— you said that yourself. Don't fuck with me, Dana. Don't fuck with me right now. I can't take much more of this shit."

"No," she protests, crawling toward me again. "It's not that at all." Her legs flank my own, and she kneels before me, running her tiny hands over my face and neck. "It's you. You're so beautiful in here." Her finger prods painfully over my heart. "You just don't want to see it."

I can't see it. I take her finger in my grasp, and gently place her hand in her lap. "You can't know me that well after a day."

Her sadness pours from her eyes in rivers. "I've seen the

absolute bottom of human nature, Sawyer. I can judge when a person is truly bad. There is only one person in this house with a soul that can't be saved, and you're not him."

Her life has only begun, not quite two decades long, and yet she has seen the kind of horror most people choose to deny exists—some of it at the hands of my father. And now, she chooses me.

Me.

"I'm not a nice person, Dana." I reach out and tug her face to mine, murmuring, "You shouldn't want me."

Her lips claim mine for a second time, her tongue eager, and her desire devouring me whole. Placing my hands on her backside, I pull her into my hard length, desperate to show her that she affects me as badly as I seem to do her. Moans escape her feverish lips, and she grinds herself into my lap.

"I don't want nice. I want what you are," she breathes.

The marble floor bites into my shoulders as I lay us back, and reach between our writhing bodies to loosen her shorts. She shimmies out of both them and her panties, the sensation of her body wriggling over mine enough to make me want to sink into her right there and then.

But she needs care. She needs at least an ounce of compassion in this fucked up arrangement.

I roll with her, placing an arm beside her head, and stroke her hair from her face with my free hand. Those damn eyes watch me with desperation, fear that I'll still reject her and push her away. My lips brush over her cheeks, and rest beside her ear as I whisper, "I might hurt you."

Warm fingers wrap around my jaw, and she cradles my face as she breathes her response. "Not by choice, though."

My father raised me with the solid belief that real men don't cry, and for thirty-one years, I haven't. But here, with a girl so broken, yet still full of heart, I weep. For all the girls I've abused in my fucked-up mental states, for the woman who gave birth to my child, and for my own mother, brutally taken from a boy who thought of her as his entire world.

I scrunch my face tight, willing the outpouring to stop, and rest my head against Dana's chest. Her hands stroke the back of my head; her fingers knit in my hair. She never speaks, but at times like this, there isn't a language on this earth that carries the right words to convey how it feels to have my crazy world shatter, and melt back together again in the warm embrace of a young woman.

My breathing eases, and I wipe away the guilty reminder of my weakness. She kisses each of my cheeks, removing the traces of moisture, and finishes with a soft, slow pull of my lip.

"You'll be okay," she assures. "Sometimes you need to break apart in order to put yourself back together stronger."

I stare into her eyes, always so expressive, and marvel at the way she manages to find the light amidst all this murky dark. "You're one of a kind—I'm fuckin' sure of it."

She twitches a smile, and I close the small gap between us to kiss her; show her that for once in my tortured, messed up head, I've found something that finally slots all the pieces into order—her.

I work my way down her slender form, placing small kisses on the hollow beneath her ribs, the point of her hips, and on each knee. Gasps fall from her lips as she writhes beneath my touch. I sit back, and take in her beauty. What I'd do to be able to spend the next few years with her, watch as she matures and her body fills out those curves. The vulnerability in her eyes as she watches me sets my chest aching anew. I smile, and lean over her to work back up her body until I reach her soft lips once more.

She runs her hands around the back of my neck, crests my shoulders, and then glides her palms over my back toward my butt. The slow exploration is heaven, sensual, and intimately erotic all at once. Resting my palm against the side of her head, I catch her gaze, and ask, "Are you sure?"

She nods. "I want it to be you."

A cry breaks free of her, echoing about the barren room as I push inside her heat. I wince at the pain she must experience with how fucking tightly her body grips my length. Dana's face contorts, and then relaxes as she opens her eyes again, smiling through her discomfort. I pull back slowly, and edge deeper on the second thrust, working her into it.

After a while of taking it slow for her sake, I smile when she pushes against me, urging me to deepen and quicken. I oblige, watching every tiny fucking detail on her beautiful face. The emotional ride she's taking is written clearly in every smile, wince, and moment of wide-eyed surprise. She pushes up on her elbows to find my mouth, kissing me deeply as her muscles begin to pulse, and pull.

We continue with only the occasional sigh or whimper from her as I stroke the hair from her face, trace her lips with my thumb, and kiss her nose, forehead, and cheeks. Her breathing grows heavy, and I close my eyes, fighting to hold on for her.

The girl falls apart beneath me, groaning through her pleasure, and crying though her laughter. I lose control, grunting through my release as my legs turn to jelly. My body weakened, I collapse over her, shifting to the side so she can breathe beneath my weight. Her leg wraps over me, and she loops her arms around my neck, kissing the top of my head.

"I knew it should be you," she whispers.

I still don't agree, but it's her body and her choice and I can be man enough to respect that.

I place an arm over her stomach and jam my hand under her side so my hold stays firm. She hums and holds me tighter, never letting go. I've never held a woman after sex, ever, but tonight it just feels so right. Comfortable and sated, I close my eyes, making the most of the moment before it comes to an end, pretending this is how things could be—always.

eggshells

"What time is it?" Dana asks sleepily. She throws an arm over her eyes and rolls towards where I kneel beside her.

"Not sure," I answer, "but I think it's late."

"Everything okay?" she asks, pulling to a sitting position and taking her crop top, which I hold out for her.

"Fine. Just figured we should probably go somewhere a bit warmer, eh?"

She nods fervently, rubbing her arms. "Totally."

I stand and wait near the door in silence as she tugs her underwear and shorts on. The house is disturbingly quiet—deathly so. Dana steps up beside me and offers a small smile, keeping her distance. I take her hand and lead the way down the hallway, out into the foyer, noting that there's no light from beneath either my father's office door or the den. In fact, there isn't a light to be seen anywhere.

"Do you think anyone's here?" Dana asks once we're safely in my room.

I pull her back into my front, running my hand in lazy circles over her stomach while I bury my face in her neck. "Not sure. It definitely seems quiet." She presses a little harder into my body, and a certain part of me awakens. "How you feeling?" I ask. "Sore?"

She shakes her head, and twists to look up at me. "Feeling pretty good. Thank you for asking."

Moments pass with her in my embrace, nothing but the rise and fall of our breathing disturbing the night. I place a palm between her legs at the apex of her thighs, the other lightly around her throat, and walk her toward the bed. She startles me from my sex-addled thoughts with a definite libido breaker.

"Do you think we should go check out the rest of the house, see if your dad has left for the night?"

"I'd rather stay right fuckin' here."

"Sawyer," she complains, turning in my grasp to face me. "What if this is our opportunity?"

So fucking what? I've just found the one thing which actually grounds me, gives me a chance at turning my shitty existence around, and she wants to go get herself killed? I think fucking not. "It might also be the perfect time to get yourself shot, sweetheart."

She slaps me on the chest, and frowns. "Come on. Where's your sense of danger, huh?" Her eyes bore into mine for a beat before she murmurs, "You tell me you're all kinds of wrong and yet you won't even try and escape your father's house."

She smirks when I take her wrists in my grasp and force her back onto the bed. Her bright eyes stare straight into the depths of my soul as I hover over her . . . just looking. "Baby, you've got no idea how wrong I am."

"Explain it to me then," she baits. "Because so far, all I've seen is a real nice guy who wouldn't hurt anyone out of turn."

My lips curl on one side, and I narrow my gaze. "You tell me, princess. What's the worst thing you think I've done?"

She rolls her eyes. "Seriously, I've seen a lot of messed up shit. Do you honestly think you can shock me with some fucking stunt you've pulled?"

"I *know* I can," I growl, pissed at her for not taking this fucking seriously. "We need to clear the air, Dana. I get what you're used to with the lifestyle, sweetheart. But you tell me—what's the worst fuckin' thing you think I could have done?"

She sits up, tucks her knees into her chest and starts counting off on her fingers. "For starters, I'd say you've done drugs, beaten somebody unconscious, shot somebody, and had an orgy with club hookers or the like."

"Standard," I say with a shrug. "What else?"

She swallows. "Murder?"

I wind my hand out between us. "And?"

Her brow furrows. "Rape?"

My hand cranks over another couple of rotations.

"Fuck, Sawyer. Torture?"

I smile. "Now you're getting warm."

"What else is there?" she asks, a little flustered.

"Armed robbery, but I was more meaning combine the last three things together and you've got what I'd call a busy fuckin' night, babe."

She frowns, but doesn't seem perturbed at all. More … disappointed. The last fucking emotion I wanted from her.

"Who?" she asks quietly. "Who did you kill?"

"All sorts."

"I meant—did you know them all? Your victims? When you say murder, you mean club hits, right?"

I shake my head slowly. "Not always."

"You killed innocent people?"

"Depends what you define as innocent."

Her throat bobs, and she frowns deeper. "Why?"

"They pissed me off, had something I wanted, or sometimes it was just for random shit," I bark out a laugh thinking about the story I'm about to tell her. "One whore, she kept on—"

Dana places her hand over my mouth. "I don't want to know."

She must have known that this is the kind of person I really am, surely. "Did you not know much about me before you got here? I thought you'd said Mel had told you stuff about me."

Her gaze slides to the far side of the room, and she shrugs. "I'd heard your name, knew who your dad is, and that you'd had some on-off thing with Mel. Other than that I'd sort of filled in the blanks with what most of the guys I've grown up around get up to."

"Nobody told you I'm crazy then?"

Her head whips about, and her jaw is set firm, her eyes dark. "You're not crazy. Don't say that."

"Gorgeous," I reply with a chuckle, "I have a fuckin' voice in my head that tells me what to do most of the time." Although he's been rather quiet lately.

"It's called your conscience," she retorts.

I snort. "Fuck, babe. This ain't a conscience. Your conscience doesn't offer suggestions on which way to cut a fuckin' asshole's throat so the blood spray doesn't get your clothes dirty."

"You expect me to believe that you've done every bad thing in your life because of some voice in your head?"

I nod.

"What's he saying now?"

Kill her . . .

Create a diversion, just like you told her to . . .

Get out of here . . .

I smile weakly at his apparent return. "Nothing just now."

She nods, and turns her attention to a loose thread on the hem of her shorts.

"Look, you get some rest on your own for a bit, okay?" I push off the bed, adjusting myself in my jeans. "I'm going to take a walk."

"Without me?"

"You want to hold it while I piss?"

She holds her hand out, pointing. "The bathroom's just there."

I look to the door opposite the bed and curse at myself. *Fucking idiot.* "Fine. I wanted to look for something in my mother's room. Forgot to do it before."

She narrows her gaze, but stays put. "You going to leave without me?"

"Fuck," I exclaim, running my hands through my hair. "No!"

"Then why are you lying to me?"

"I just want you to stay put."

"Why?" she yells.

"Why not?" I holler back. "Why can't you just do as you're fuckin' told?"

Her face twists, and she opens her mouth to speak, but chooses against it. I sigh as she shunts herself roughly under the covers, and yanks the sheet over her shoulder. "Go. Fuck off then."

"I just need time alone to think, Dana. Nothing on you."

"It's never anything to do with me unless people need something."

Where the fuck did that come from? What does she want me to do? Fucking propose so she knows it wasn't just a meaningless fuck?

Choosing to ignore her temper tantrum for now, I snatch up my T-shirt and tug it on as I head down the hallway. She had a point back there before things turned ugly—it *is* unusually quiet, and perhaps there is some loophole for us tonight. But that doesn't mean I want her snooping around a house she isn't familiar with, trying to find an out—not when I know the place like the back of my hand.

I'd rather do it myself and know she's out of harm's way until I need her.

First stop, I check out the kitchen and staffroom. Both come up empty and darker than a coal pit. I swing past my father's office and den one more time, opening each door just to be sure. Nothing. The whole house—all twenty thousand-square feet of it—comes up emptier than a nun's womb.

Standing in the library, the final room I've checked, I take a look outside at the gatehouse. The lights are on, and I can see the shadow of a man in the control room. Still, the whole situation seems off. Why would my old man leave us here relatively unguarded? What could be so important that he's left the property, and most importantly, how long will he be gone?

I leave the library, shutting the door behind me, and head for my room again when a torchlight snaps on, stopping me in my tracks. The beam blinds me for a moment, and I raise a hand to see who's shining it at me.

"You're required in the pool-house."

The pool-house. Of course.

I nod at Gregory, one of the long-serving guards, and follow him out over the back patio to the dark building. My gut churns, and my palms are slick. Something feels off about the whole situation. The low murmur of voices breaks the night as Gregory opens the door and ushers me inside.

In the far corner are my father and one of his guards I remember, but can't place the name of. The table they're at has a sole lantern in the center, which provides a dim highlight on the surrounding area. My old man ushers me over, and I take a seat opposite the mystery guy.

"What's going on?" I ask.

"Where the fuck were you?" my father hisses. "I had the staff look for you, but they couldn't find either you or your whore."

Of course—the staff aren't allowed in the north wing. "I was in Mom's room."

"Both of you?" He looks . . . hurt.

"Yeah. So?"

His nostrils flare, obvious even in the dull light. "Find what you were looking for?"

"Not sure yet." I grab the bottle of scotch in front of him, the tumbler, and pour myself a glass. "Why are you all out here?"

"Perry and I were mid-meeting and next thing you know I've got Gregory telling me that I'm down a few members of staff." *Perry.* The hard-faced asshole glares at me while my old man continues, "Turns out there's a sniper positioned somewhere along the front fence. So naturally, we're out here, out of view until the bastard is located and what staff I have left give me a reason to pay them this month."

I lift an eyebrow. "What about the guy in the gatehouse?"

"Dead."

"Did you put an extra in the crow's nest?"

He eyeballs me. "Why are you asking me this?"

"Curious," I shrug.

My old man's gaze narrows. "Of course I put an extra up there. Although, the asshole barely lasted ten minutes."

Fuck me. Somebody's got serious grief with the old man— not that it's surprising after what went down today. "You think you finally fucked up this time?" I do my best to act nonchalant as my head calculates the likelihood of Dana staying put until I get back to her.

"As if I'd tell you." His distrust is evident in his eyes.

I look away before he sees right through my plan, and take the tumbler in hand. His drink burns through to my gut, and I place the empty glass down with a clunk. "Guess I better go get your collateral before she does somethin' stupid like get shot." My father continues to eye me as I stand. "Oh, wait," I say sarcastically, "she already has."

"You have five minutes to drag her slutty ass in here before I send Gregory after you." He gestures to one of his staff for a clean glass. "Don't fuck it up."

I flip him the middle finger, and walk out of the pool-house and, all going to plan, out of his fucking life.

75

opportunity knocks

If I said my heart didn't race when I stepped into my room to find it empty, it would be a bald-faced lie. It fuckin' well near broke the land-speed record. The bed is rumpled, but vacant, and her boots are still tossed where she threw them this morning—beside the chair.

Panicked and angry, I turn to head out and hunt for her when I hear a slight, but very clear sniffle.

The bathroom. Of course. Where else do girls hide out when they're angry?

"You still fuckin' angry?" I stomp over to the doorway, ready to pick her up and carry her out if necessary. Who knows if we'll get another opportunity like this? Barely one step into the room I still as my breath catches.

She sits on the basin, the mirror on the cabinet behind her smashed. Pieces lie over the floor like a carpet of glitter as they catch the light flowing in from the bedroom. "I screwed up, Sawyer." She cradles her left hand in her lap, blood staining her shorts as it runs from between her fingers. "I really screwed up."

"What the fuck is this?" I ask quietly. "What did you do?"

"I was so angry at you," she sobs while I carefully approach her. "I came in here after you left and got fucked off with my reflection." She lets out a nervous chuckle, and allows me take her hands in mine to look at the wound. "I punched the mirror and did this."

My chest tightens when she lifts her fingers to reveal a jagged gash on her wrist. The rest of her right hand is slashed as well, but nothing is bleeding quite like this.

"I'm scared," she tells me. "I've never bled like this before."

She has a damn right to be fucking scared—she's done the equivalent of slashing her wrist.

"There's first aid in the staffroom." I snatch a towel off the rack, wrap it tightly about her arm, and pull it hard. "Here. Place your hand over this and press."

"What are you going to do?" she asks through her hiccups.

"Fix you up." What else?

Her chin quivers, and the corners of her mouth are downturned, same as her gaze. She's ashamed of her mistake. I can see it. I know how it feels. "I just snapped," she says. "Everything welled up, and I just snapped without thinking about the consequence."

"Don't beat yourself up over it, though" I tell her. "We all lose control sometimes, and every now and then, this kind of shit happens because of it. I've been there, done it plenty of fuckin' times."

She sighs, and smiles. "Yeah, I bet you have." It's no more than a few words said in humor, but it speaks volumes.

As I help her off the basin I fight the lava coursing my veins at my realization. For once in my fucking life, I've made someone calm—I've been the cause of comfort, not pain.

What the fuck else is this girl capable of?

•• • ••

Dana walks behind me as I head for the staffroom in the darkness. She still has the towel pressed to her wrist, and the green color is slowly turning an interesting shade of pink. I won't lie; I'm freaking the fuck out. It's always been me who's been injured, and always been one of the brothers who've stitched me up. I've never hung around to see how the people I've hurt have dealt with this shit. I don't have a fucking clue what I'm doing, but I'll sure as hell give it a go.

She flops onto a sofa while I hunt through the cupboards, looking for the first-aid kit. On the fourth try I find the right door, and snatch the kit from its position front and center on the shelf. Her head is resting on the back of the sofa when I spin around, and even with next to no light, I can see she doesn't look very good.

"Feeling faint?" I ask.

She nods.

"Won't be long and we'll have that sorted," I say, grabbing her under an arm to hoist her up. "Off to the kitchen now."

"Why?"

"You'll see."

I help her cross the hallway, and push through the swing door into the industrial-style kitchen. Dana leans a hip into the counter while I open the kit and hunt through for what I need. The moonlight is minimal, and if I'm to have a hope of getting this right I'm going to need more light. There's no way I'm flicking the overhead lights on though. May as well stick a fucking beacon out the window for whoever's shoots up the guards.

"You want to know why I was coming back to get you?" I ask in the hope of distracting her from passing out.

"Not really," she says with a weak chuckle.

"Well," I answer, heading to the pantry for the emergency torch I've seen in there, "you're going to find out." I grab a couple of chocolate biscuits while I'm at it, and take them and the torch over to where she stands. I twist the lantern-style light on, and place it beside the kit. Grabbing Dana round the waist, I hoist her on to the counter. "Eat these." I pass her the biscuits to chew on while I yank drawers open until I find the cutlery, and pull out a butter knife. "I was heading back to get you and leave."

"What?" she asks groggily, her head lolling back against the wall. "You keep telling me we can't."

"I know what I fuckin' said." The gas stove fires with a click, and I crank the dial around to its hottest setting. "But you were right before; tonight is our chance."

"What you doing?"

"Best you don't think about it," I reply, wrapping a dishcloth around the handle of the knife. "Take that towel off your arm." I run the tap over the sink, and half fill it with cold water.

Dana fumbles with the blood-soaked fabric and reveals her wrist. It's bleeding as quickly as it did the minute she sliced it. I take a deep breath, and blot at the wound to figure out where most of the blood is coming from.

"Hold this back over it for a moment," I say, passing her the towel.

She complies, and I pick up the wrapped knife. Holding the exposed end in the center of the gas flame, I wait while the metal heats. It glows a dull orange, and the heat transferring through the cloth to my hand is already uncomfortable. Switching hands repeatedly, I persist until the end glows close to red-hot.

"Drop the towel. Actually ... take it off your arm, but you better bite down on it so you don't lose your fuckin' tongue."

Dana follows orders slowly, barely getting the towel between her teeth before her head drops back again. With my shoulder into her chest, and holding her good arm back with my body, I lean my weight into her and touch the red-hot knife to the wound. It sizzles and cracks, and the smell of burning flesh is enough to make me hurl if I weren't so focused on the job at hand.

She screams, the towel drops from her mouth, and any trace of grogginess has left her as she struggles against me. "Motherfucker!" she finally manages to get out as her initial shock wears off.

I toss the knife into the sink, and wait for her flesh to cool while she dry-retches. Retrieving the cloth that I had wrapped around the knife, I dab the wet fabric over her newly cauterized wound and clear off the old blood. Nothing springs forth.

For once in my life, it appears I've done something right.

"We'll get this fixed up properly later, but for now, at least you won't bleed out while we get the fuck outta here."

Dana offers me a weak smile, and brushes her fingers

around the outside of the reddened flesh. "Hope you boys like a good scar as much as us girls do." She laughs quietly, and then sighs, a lonely, resigned sound.

"Finish your biscuit," I say, pulling a bandage from the kit. "Just got to cover it and then we're out of here. The guards out back are going to know where to find us after that howl."

"Couldn't really help it," she says dryly.

"I know." She's a fucking trooper for getting through that with only a scream and near vomiting. I half expected her to pass out. The woman just won't stop fucking amazing me.

Dana watches keenly while I clean the last of the blood away, dry the area and apply an adhesive bandage over the puckered, angry flesh. Her free hand covers mine, and she stills my movements. "Thank you."

"You won't be doing something that fuckin' stupid again in a hurry." I realize how bad it sounds the minute I finish the last word. Her hand retracts, and her head dips. "Never mind," I say, a bit lighter, and gently pat her cheek with my palm. "Can't change the past."

She smiles and nods. "No, we can't."

My mind's set—I have to get her out of here. I can't fuck up this time. Never have I met a girl with this much strength and determination. She's been kidnapped, had her old man die in her arms, and caused herself a life-threatening injury, but through it all she never quit. She just kept going. If I could get her on my bike, and my patch on her ass, we'd be fucking unstoppable. The shit we could achieve together ...

"Come on." I help her down, and grab the torch. "I'll show you a little secret."

I've got to make this woman mine.

the great escape

"I've lost track of where we are in this place," Dana says, holding the back of my shirt so she doesn't get lost in the dark. "Why can't we use the torch anymore?"

"Because directly across the courtyard is where my old man is."

"Oh," she replies simply.

The dull murmuring of voices stills me in my travels, and we wait in silence while I work out where they're coming from. Two of the guards are tucked mostly out of view behind a stand of palms, sharing a cigarette. I reach back, and give her a little tug so she starts to move with me again.

We edge our way through the house, and reach the long corridor, which looks over the pool area. I try the door I need, and find it's locked. "Fuck," I hiss under my breath.

"What?" she whispers.

"Nothing. Just means we need to take the long way, which means back-tracking."

I lead us back the way we've just come, and stop two doors down. Thankfully the handle turns in my grasp otherwise this master plan of mine could have done what I do best—failed. I open the door and the immediate scent of my mother hits me—gardenias. As suspected, the reading room is untouched, still looking as if she'd up and walked out of here mere hours ago. My father mustn't have been in here since he shut the north wing off if her perfume still clings to every worn chair, and bound book.

Odd.

"Wow, it's nice in here." Dana looks around in the dull moonlight, and brushes her fingertips over the open pages of a novel on the table beside my mother's armchair. "So different to the rest of the place."

"It was my mother's favorite place to be," I inform her reluctantly, looking around the window for the latch. "It's kind of special to me."

"I can see why."

"Let's get movin'," I say sharply and flick the catch, sliding the sash window open.

Dana steps up, and slides a leg out over the sill as voices echo up the corridor. She freezes, and I move to cover her while we listen.

"He should have been outside a long time ago," my father shouts.

"Sir, it's not safe for you to be on your—"

"I wouldn't be on my own, Gregory, if you bastards did your job properly."

"Perhaps I could—"

"You are *not* allowed in this part of the house, now or ever. Go! Get out of my fucking sight."

Rapid footfalls echo toward us. I spin, and shove Dana to get her to move. She scrambles her other leg out, wincing at the pressure on her arm, and leaps off into the garden below. I follow suit, climbing onto the sill and swearing quietly when my cut catches the latch. The footfalls stop, and a low chuckle replaces them.

"Oh dear. The rabbit's caught in the snare. How unfortunate . . . for you"

The leather doesn't give as I yank furiously at it. *Fuck.* There's no way in hell I'm leaving my colors behind.

"Where you going, boy?"

"Out." The cut comes free with a jerk, and I slip my other leg out.

"You step one foot off this property, I'll fucking hunt you down and kill you," my father screams after us. "Get the fuck back here!"

Dana steps aside as I push off, and I land in the garden beside her. "Run for that gazebo," I say, pointing to the far right corner of the yard. "Don't stop."

She breaks into a long stride, and I turn to see my father's foot coming through the window. "You come out here and you're dead, you fuckwit," I yell up at him. "Did you forget why you were hiding out back like a motherfucking pussy to begin with?"

"I'll take my chances," he growls, positioning to jump.

Fucker's crazy. Guess it is hereditary.

I turn and take after Dana, cursing the heavy boots that were most definitely designed for riding, not running. We cover gray, shadowy ground, nearing the halfway mark when I'm acutely aware of my old man's presence behind me. My chances of out-running the old man are near to none. He was always a stickler for fitness, and I could guarantee the bastard still runs five miles every morning. Years of heavy drinking, cigarettes, and drugs catch up to me, and my lungs burn for air.

Still, I push on, just like Dana does.

"Stop!" A guard sprints towards us, and catches Dana mid-flight as she tries to dodge him. "It's not secure."

A crack rings out over the grounds, and the guard falls to the grass while Dana screams, scrambling free of his limp arm. His blood covers the side of her face, and she breaks into a run again, still crying.

I slow to a jog as I approach the guy, but his face is now plastered across a square foot of the lawn. There's no coming back for him. Picking up pace again, I steal a glance over my shoulder and see my father mere feet from catching up. My heavy shoes leave dents in the lawn as I sprint toward the gazebo, and the hidden access to the crow's nest.

"To the left, Dana!" I holler as she reaches the painted building.

"You won't make it," my father yells. "You're fooling yourself!"

I reach the side of the gazebo, and thrust my hand through the ivy to find the handle. The loud resonating sound of a pistol firing precedes a sharp sting in my shoulder, and I lurch away from the door, cursing as it burns.

"Leave us alone," Dana screams at my old man as he points his gun toward her. "Haven't you done enough?"

"Apparently not," he says, advancing.

I dive in front of Dana, but it's too late. *Crack*. She whelps, and looks down in shock, clutching at her stomach.

"Why do you always run, Sawyer?" my father says with a

sigh, ignoring her moans. "Now look what you've made me do."

I push my weakened hand through the ivy again, and wrench the door to the stairwell open. Snatching Dana by her shirt, I try to shove her through, but she stands firm, eyes pleading with me. "No, Sawyer."

"Just go!" I scream at her, frustrated, upset…*feeling*. "Go."

She shakes her head, and looks at me with the saddest fucking eyes as blood trickles from the corner of her beautiful lips.

"No," I wail in broken chords, disbelieving, angered, and begging with my devil for a fucking answer to this.

But he doesn't say a thing.

He's not even there.

"Isn't this tragic?" my father says with a chuckle. "Romeo and fucking Juliet. Who wants to go first?"

I turn to him, planning on the ways I'll make his sorry ass suffer, and ready to die in the process. "We go, you go too, asshole."

He lifts an eyebrow, and then throws his back and laughs: loud, obnoxious and arrogant. But it's all a ploy. As with every-fucking-thing he's done with me in my life, it's calculated. Planned to the last detail.

I move to disarm him while he's distracted, but the asshole is anything but. His eyes snap into focus, dark and determined as I step forward. My life slows, becoming a reel of painful, pathetic images—a montage to my time as a failure. He leans right, points the pistol around behind me, and fires.

Hot, unrelenting panic washes through me from head to

toe.

Dana hits the ground face-first in a mess of blonde hair and gore. My ears pound and the pressure in my skull is unbearable. The bastard who gave me life, just to ruin it and revel in doing so, smiles with the same sick pride he showed the news story in his office.

The devil skids into position, apologizing for his absence, and we get to work on making my every fantasy a reality. Crimson droplets rain over the pale-green lawn as my fist connects with the fucker's face. My old man staggers back, and the same manic determination alights his eyes. Neither of us have a single ounce of fucking control left—it's all in, no holds barred.

Armageddon on a front lawn.

"You know, I tried with you, Sawyer," he bellows, "I really did. I wanted so badly for you to prove yourself, to show you were brought into my life for a reason, but you've failed. I've failed." He trains the gun on my head, and shrugs. "You were a mistake at the start, and it seems you'll be a mistake at the end."

"I'm not a mistake, old man. I'm just not you."

I can't say exactly what happens in those next minutes. All I know is that one minute I was facing down the barrel of my father's gun, and the next we were scrapping like two rabid dogs on the lawn. There comes a point in rage or madness that when crossed, results in the parts of a brain which control reason and logic shutting down. An animal instinct takes over and the brain redirects focus to the base functions of maiming and killing. There was blood, there were breaking bones, and even flesh torn from bodies by teeth.

It was ugly, it was primal, and it was fucking beautiful.

All until the motherfucking cavalry arrived. My surroundings scream back into clarity with a deafening roar as two guards sprint from the house. My focus is broken long enough for my father to collect me square in the jaw, and I reel back with the hit. He lunges for his pistol, which lies on the lawn at our feet, but another crack echoes around the grounds and he falls back on his ass, clutching his arm.

The guards bear down on us, their own pieces raised in response. I've got mere seconds before I join Dana on the dirt. As my old man makes a feeble move to retrieve his gun, I turn and scramble to her lifeless body. With my breath jerking into my lungs in short bursts, I push enough bloody hair free of her face to reveal one of her perfect green eyes. It stares aimlessly across the grounds, but still so bright. I whisper my apologies and lay a kiss to her forehead. "I'm so fucking sorry, baby. I promise I'll make this right. I just . . . I can't do it tonight." I swallow hard—twice—before I can continue. "You've changed me, baby, and I'll always love you for that."

Shouting and cursing echoes off the stone wall as I dart into the stairwell that leads to the crow's nest. My father is screaming at his staff, and ordering my 'head on a fucking platter'. I scramble up the steel steps, grunting and moaning at the pain spiking throughout my body. My knuckles are swollen and bruised, my arm bleeding in places where the skin hangs loosely, and a warm trickle runs constantly down the collar of my T-shirt.

I reach the top and come to an immediate halt, staring over the edge at the drop to the ground. But it's not the fall that has me worried—it's the dozen or so Fallen Aces looking up at me for answers. One more than the others.

"Where the fuck is my sister?" Hooch yells.

I look down at Judas's son, the VP of the southern chapter, and the only remaining member of his family, and choke. Boots pound the steps behind me, and I steal a glance at the access ladder. I want to explain it all, tell him everything, but there's no time.

Several of the men below startle as I place a boot on the ledge, and nod tightly at them. "If any of you fuckers wanted to be world-class ball players, now's the time to practice your catching." I swing my back foot forward, and step off, hoping to land on my back.

My body lands on the leafy dirt with a sickening crunch. I'm fighting for air, and the world spins about me in a haze of grey, black, and orange. Hooch moves into my line of sight, his imposing stature towering over me as I struggle to work out whether it's safe to move, or if I'll be stuck in a wheelchair for the rest of my days. The bastard really does take after his father, right down to the beard.

His angry glare connects with my gaze, and I wilt as the understanding reads clear as day in his dark eyes. His nostrils flare, a slight twitch jerks underneath one eye, and he swallows slowly. I'm mentally preparing for the end, certain he's going to pull his piece and take me out there and then, but the fucker throws me a curveball.

"Get up. We need to hustle if you want a chance at growin' old." He straightens, and turns to one of his men while I groan to a seated position. "Jo-Jo, he's your bitch."

Yeah, and he's nothing but a fuck-up . . .

Continue with

DEVIL IN THE DETAIL

Ty & Ramona's story

Continue with Ty's story,

DEVIL IN THE DETAIL

One look, one touch, and I can breath again. But Ramona's not mine to have. She's old lady to a member of the Fallen Saints MC. And not just any brother—he's the most psychotic man I've ever known.

Yet, I want her. I have to have her.

Foolish? Maybe. Selfish? Definitely. But nothing can stop me proving she needs this.

•••

Prefer to binge read?

You can read the entire *Butcher Boys Series* in one set!
https://books2read.com/ButcherBoys

•••

Like to know more about the Fallen Aces MC?

Grab the first three in the series today:
https://books2read.com/FallenAcesMC

•••

Want to hang out with like-minded chicks?

Jump into **Max's Minxes** on Facebook!

Also by Max

STANDALONE
Malaise
Tough Love
Echoes in the Storm
Black Whole Heart

ARCADIA HIGH ANARCHISTS (Mature YA)
High Horse • Good Girls • Bad Boys • Rich Riot
Loyal Love • Done Deal

DARK TIDE (Rock Star) SERIES
Down Beat • Amplifier • Bottleneck •Fulcrum

TWISTED HEARTS (Age Gap)
Desire • Regret • Trust

BUTCHER BOYS (Suspense) SERIES
Devil You Know • Devil on Your Back
Devil May Care • Devil in the Detail • Devil Smoke

FALLEN ACES MC SERIES
Unrequited • Unbreakable • Tormented
Existential • Misguided • Redundant

www.maxhenryauthor.com/the-books

Sign up for the latest news and updates!

www.maxhenryauthor.com/newsletter

The Music

"Never Seen Runaway" – Jay Kill, The Hustle Standard
"Raise Hell" – Brandi Carlile
"What Makes A Man" – City and Colour
"Save Me" – Listenbee, Naz Tokio
"Free Bird" – Lynyrd Skynyrd
"I Could Die For You" – Red Hot Chili Peppers
"Teardrop" – Massive Attack
"Hallelujah" – Jeff Buckley
"Riverside" – Agnes Obel
"Save Me" – Moxi
"Wicked Game" – Chris Issak
"Stay" – Thirty Seconds to Mars
"Walk on Water" – Kat Dahlia
"Elastic Heart" – Sia
"Talking to a Stranger" – Birds of Tokyo
"Brother, Do You Know the Road?" – Hiss Golden
Messenger
"Heart Shaped Box" – Ásgeir
"We Never Change" – Coldplay
"Breathe Me" – Sia
"Snap Your Fingers, Snap Your Neck" – Prong
"Break Stuff"– Limp Bizkit
"People = Shit" – Slipknot

About the Author

Born and raised in Canterbury, New Zealand, Max now resides with her family in beautiful and sunny Queensland, Australia.

Life with two young children can be hectic at times and, although she may not write as often as she would like, Max wouldn't change a thing.

An avid lover of stories from a young age, she enjoys nothing more than to get lost in the pages while the characters dictate what direction she takes. Her favourite genre to write is young/new adult and the events in her stories may or may not be related to real life experiences (only she will ever know for sure).

In her down time, Max can be found at her local gym brainstorming through a session with the weights. If not, she's probably out drooling over one of many classic cars on show that she wishes she owned.

Be Sure to Follow Her at:

Amazon

http://amazon.com/author/maxhenry

TikTok & Instagram

@maxhenryauthor

www.tiktok.com/maxhenryauthor

www.instagram.com/maxhenryauthor

Facebook

www.facebook.com/MaxHenryAuthor

Goodreads

www.goodreads.com/author/show/
7555353.Max_Henry

Bookbub

www.bookbub.com/authors/max-henry

**For ALL updates and announcements
– sign up to Max's e-mail list:**

www.maxhenryauthor.com/newsletter

**And for exclusive news and excerpts,
join Max's reader group, the Minxes!**

www.facebook.com/groups/346994535466425/

www.ingramcontent.com/pod-product-compliance
Lightning Source LLC
Chambersburg PA
CBHW052109150726

48002CB00006B/2276